Recommendations for *Chloe*

"Cheryl Chumley provides in her Chloe's People series a much-needed bridge over the gap separating the faith community and the secular world. For too long, many in the church community have lived in a bubble, leaving out those who most need to hear biblical truths. And they've done so because of a basic lack of understanding of what makes men turn to alcohol; why women become prostitutes; how children are led into gangs and drugs; and worse. After all, it's difficult for someone raised in the church surrounded by family members who are supportive and loving to truly understand why a young college girl, for example, would choose to pose naked in *Playboy* rather than earn her money as a waitress. But the Great Commission requires we reach out to these fallen, these non-believers, these sin-filled, and to guide them to the hope of the cross and teach them about the miracle of grace. We just have to know how to communicate with them. The stories of Chloe's People are gritty enough to resonate with the unbeliever, and biblically inspired enough to touch the heart of the believer, with the end result being a powerful cultural tool to advance the glory of God and His message of redemption."

—Mike Huckabee, former governor of Arkansas
and host of *Huckabee* on TBN

"One of a Christian's biggest challenges is to reach out with compassion and love to those who seem unlovable. *Chloe* tells a sad but realistic story of how people can become an 'unlovable' in the first place, and in the end, gives readers who are already saved by Christ an eye-opener in how to better share the gospel with those who are not."

—Troy Miller, CEO National Religious Broadcasters

"Sometimes fiction is able to communicate truth to a general audience better than Truth itself. In *Chloe*, Cheryl Chumley uses this vehicle to drive home some truth that especially parents of daughters and church leaders should read."

—Cal Thomas, syndicated columnist

"A fast-moving fictional story of a little girl's challenges, *Chloe* carries a powerful non-fiction punch: how God saves even those who seem beyond saving."

—Sam Sorbo, actress and host of *The Sam Sorbo Show*

CHLOE

BOOK ONE OF CHLOE'S PEOPLE

CHLOE

A NOVEL

CHERYL CHUMLEY

FIDELIS
PUBLISHING

Fidelis Publishing ®
Winchester, VA • Nashville, TN
www.fidelispublishing.com

ISBN: 9781956454598
ISBN: 9781956454604 (ebook)

Chloe: A Novel
Book One of the Series Chloe's People

Scripture used in this book comes from the following translations:
    (NIV) New International Version®, NIV® Scripture comes from Holy Bible, Copyright ©1973, 1978, 1984, 2011 by Biblica, Inc.® Used by permission. All rights reserved worldwide.
    (ESV) English Standard Version - The Holy Bible, English Standard Version. ESV® Text Edition: 2016. Copyright © 2001 by Crossway Bibles, a publishing ministry of Good News Publishers.
    (NKJV) Scripture taken from the New King James Version®. Copyright © 1982 by Thomas Nelson. Used by permission. All rights reserved.
    (KJV) King James Version is in the public domain.

Order at www.faithfultext.com for a significant discount. Email info@fidelis publishing.com to inquire about bulk purchase discounts.

Cover designed by Diana Lawrence
Interior design by Lisa Parnell
Edited by Amanda Varian

Manufactured in the United States of America

10 9 8 7 6 5 4 3 2 1

FIDELIS
PUBLISHING

For you were once darkness,
but now you are light in the Lord.
Live as children of light.

—EPHESIANS 5:8

CHAPTER ONE

"One, two, three, four . . ."

Chloe shuffled down the aisle, letting her finger-tips graze the smooth vinyl of the seats as she passed while marking each one with a quiet count. The bus was empty and she didn't have to worry about her book bag bouncing off someone's head, so she let it bang on the back of the seats, whispering softly with each thump.

"Five, six, seven . . ."

Her progress to the exit was slow and the driver shot her a look of disapproval, but Chloe kept her head down, pretending not to notice. It was a free country. Chloe could sit anywhere she wanted, and where she liked best was the last seat of the bus.

Nobody bothered her there—and besides, it gave the best view of all the other drivers on the road. Chloe would often watch their faces and try to imagine what they were thinking, where they were going, what kind of family they had. And if they had kids in the back seat, Chloe would try and get them to stick out their tongues when nobody was looking.

Then she would feel bad because she would remember how her own mother once slapped her for sticking out her tongue at a stranger on a bus. She could still recall his face . . . his scrunched nose and crinkled eyes and grimaced

1

mouth, and the way he shoved his face hard against the glass of the back door on the bus, his features squished into a clownish arrangement.

For two stoplights, Chloe tried to ignore him, stealing sidewise glances at her mother before flicking cautious eyes at him. For two stoplights, she struggled to keep from laughing out loud. But then he pushed his beanie cap high on his head so his bald forehead seemed huge and at the same time, reached for the corners of his mouth with two fingers and pulled wide, exposing a missing tooth on the left side where the incisor should have been—and that's when Chloe lost it. She guffawed and for one tragic moment, forgot where she was. She scrunched her own face as tightly as she could, then stuck out her tongue.

It was at that moment her mother had turned her head and looked. With a shout of anger, she pulled her right hand from the steering wheel and slapped Chloe in the face with the back of her hand. Reflexively, Chloe closed her teeth hard, biting her tongue before she was able to draw it back fully into her mouth. The final scene of the drama was the comically wide eyes and open mouth of the man as he stared in astonishment. Chloe caught his expression but dropped her head in embarrassment before their eyes could meet. The taste of blood had filled her mouth as she rolled her sore tongue around her cheeks and kept silent the rest of the ride home.

Now, as she ticked off the count of green vinyl, she wondered idly what became of that man and if he ever again made faces at little kids through the window on the back of the bus.

"Eight, nine, ten . . ." Chloe whispered, thumping her backpack one last time and reaching for the pole at the top of the stairs.

The bus driver was glaring at her now but Chloe took her time descending the steps, feeling the frigid winter air on her face through the open door and pausing to adjust her sock before jumping lightly to the snowy dust covering of the pavement. She took an extra second to pull her hand clear of the door. He could just wait. There was no law, after all, about sitting in the back of the bus. She pretended not to notice as he slammed the door hard and peeled from the curb.

She waited until he was several seconds down the road before she shrugged her shoulders hard, trying to reposition the backpack so the straps wouldn't cut through her coat so harshly to her shoulder blades. *That dang Mrs. Hatcheck, always giving homework, always making the class take two, even three, books home to do the assignments. Why did English have to be such a pain?* Chloe shrugged again, and suddenly her shoulder was free.

The strap broke.

With an exasperated shout, Chloe tossed her bag to the ground and yanked off her green knit mittens. The cold swirled around her hands and she fumbled to find enough slack in the strap to tie a knot. An image of her mother's angry face flashed across her mind and Chloe grunted with effort, trying to rush the job. One more late day and she would be grounded for a week.

"Son of a —!" Chloe clamped her lips before the word escaped, but she repeated with emphasis, watching helplessly as the cloth slipped from her grip. Again, Chloe grasped the ties and worked to form a knot, but her fingers were too cold and the length of the straps too short. She didn't dare waste any more time. She scooped up her bag and wrapped her arms around it tightly, huffing at its heaviness as she walked quickly, too quickly for the weather conditions.

CHLOE

Rounding the corner on Stefania Street, her feet slipped in the slushy snow of the sidewalk and down she went. This time, she didn't even try to stop the expletives pouring from her lips. A passing woman shot a shocked glance, but Chloe didn't care. She was too busy watching her bag slide across the walk and into the street, where a passing car promptly sloshed it with muddy water. She let loose another string of curses, watching with a stab of glee when the same woman who just passed stopped to stare. Chloe stared right back and slowly, deliberately, raised a middle finger. She snickered as the woman hurried away. Then gingerly she sat up and stretched her sore leg. Her pants were soaked through and she shivered as cold seeped onto her skin.

"Well now, little child, that's some vocabulary you've got there. But tell me, do you need some help?"

Surprised, Chloe looked toward the voice.

Standing before her was perhaps the most wrinkled face she had ever seen, topped by perhaps the largest black rim of a hat she had ever seen, and for a moment, she wanted to laugh. But her amusement soon gave way to wonder as she caught a glimpse of ice blue eyes peering down at her, and the more she looked, the more she wondered, and the more she wondered, the more she felt herself drawn deep into the blue. The eyes seemed to give off sparks of white and gold and for a second, a brief second, an image of tiny dancing angels with fluttering golden wings flashed across Chloe's mind. Then she blinked and the eyes were blue again, but warm, not icy, and as they swept over her, the cold in her legs disappeared and a light tingle, almost a tickle, swept her skin. She giggled at the sensation.

Then immediately, she felt embarrassed and looked away.

"That's quite a sad fall for a birthday girl to take," he said, extending an impossibly large hand to Chloe. His smile was gleaming and Chloe couldn't help but respond with a smile of her own. He seemed so familiar, yet he was a stranger. She took his hand and pulled herself to her feet, forgetting for the moment the soreness in her hip.

"How'd you know it was my birthday?"

For answer, he pointed. Chloe followed his finger to her backpack, still laying in the street. The zipper was split, exposing several of the contents to the wet elements. The man walked over and retrieved her bag, holding up a brightly colored card with the words "You're 9!" emblazoned on the front. It was a card from Chloe's favorite teacher, Mrs. Hamptree. Chloe loved math, and Mrs. Hamptree loved teaching math. It was a match made in heaven.

"This is yours, is it not, Chloe?" He wiped it on his jacket before dropping it into her bag. She watched as he deftly tied together her broken straps and with a couple of tugs, zipped it closed.

Chloe nodded, then blurted, "But how'd you know my name's Chloe?"

He cocked his head to the side and his blue eyes flashed with humor. "Well, this is yours too, isn't it?" He shook the bag slightly and Chloe looked at the flap of cloth. In big block letters drawn with a black magic marker was written CHLOE RICHARDS. It was a class rule all students must write their names on the outsides of their backpacks. Chloe took her bag without saying a word.

"Now shall we get you home?" He proffered his left arm and with his right, tapped the tip of an umbrella gently on the ground. Immediately, a massive bowl of bright blue cloth spread before them and the man, with a swift, smooth movement, lifted it above their heads. The umbrella was large enough to cover them both, and then some. In fact, it was the largest umbrella Chloe ever saw and she was about to ask about it when she heard the pitter-patter of tiny droplets. He opened his umbrella just in time. In fact, he opened it just *before* time, and Chloe scrunched her face in wonder, trying now to remember if he had the umbrella in his hand when he first approached and if so, why she hadn't noticed it.

"Are you coming?" His voice was deep, but soft, like the echo of a whisper, and it was strangely comforting to Chloe. She thought she knew him from somewhere, but where? She scrunched her eyes and searched his face for clues.

He just smiled down at her and bent his arm, signaling for her to take ahold.

"It's mighty slippery out there and this rain is more ice than water." The drops smacked louder against the umbrella, bouncing into the distance rather than soaking into the cloth.

Chloe gazed into his face and saw, with some shock, his wrinkles were gone. Then he shifted and a ray of light broke through the clouds and beamed on them both, just for a second, and the age lines were back, etching his forehead and crisscrossing his cheeks like the wandering lines of a toddler-sized artist. Chloe blinked once, twice, then shrugged. *It must have been the light*, she decided, taking his arm and wondering once again, as they set off, just where she knew him from and when it was they previously met. She wanted to ask but felt it might somehow be rude. After all, he seemed to know her so well.

"Now tell me three things you learned in school today. And did Mrs. Hamptree give you back your quiz grade?"

"How do you know I had a math quiz today?" Chloe looked up in surprise.

"Math teachers always give quizzes. Don't they?"

She thought for a second. "Yeah, they do." Then she chuckled. "But I like them. They're so easy. I got an 'A' on this one. It was a 98, really. That's an 'A.'"

Chloe smiled proudly and gave a little skip, grabbing tighter to her escort's hand as her foot slipped on the slush.

"But I would've had a 100 if I didn't write so messy and put a six at the end when I meant a five," she said, warming to her subject. "I did the whole problem right, but then in the answer I put six by mistake. But Mrs. Hamptree only marked me off two points for that 'cause she could see by my work that I knew what I was doing. That's why I like Mrs. Hamptree."

She glanced at his face. His blue eyes shined bright, urging her to continue.

"If you show her the work," she said, her words like a flow of water suddenly released from a spigot, "she only takes off points from where you go wrong, and not the whole thing. So if a problem's worth five points, and you go through the steps and it's like step three where you get it wrong, she'll still give you a couple points for getting it right up until step three. That's a good way to do it." Chloe nodded for emphasis.

"Last year, Mr. Bache used to grade it all wrong if you got the answer wrong. Even if you got everything else right, but then had messy writing or something, and wrote six when you knew it was five. With him, you had to get the answer right no matter what, and he didn't care about seeing your work at all. You didn't get any points for getting any of the steps right. It was either all right or all wrong. I think that's stupid, don't you? Don't you think so?"

She looked at his face for confirmation.

His teeth flashed white against the gray winter sky. But instead of answering, he said, "So you like your math teacher this year."

"Oh, I love Mrs. Hamptree." Chloe stopped short and looked him in the eye. She paused, taking in the deep blue and glints of light. "Hey, you want to see something?" She didn't wait for an answer but slipped her backpack off her shoulder. "Want to see what she gave me for my birthday?"

With a quick slip of her fingers, Chloe unzipped her outside pocket and pulled forth a shiny object. She held it out for him to see. Gently, he reached with a long finger and tapped the dangling object. It was a small silver Eiffel Tower figurine attached to a round clip.

"It's a key chain," Chloe said proudly. "And look. Look here."

She held the tower closer up toward his face and ran her thumbnail along the base, revealing as she did five small block letters etched into the metal.

"See? Can you see that?"

"D-R-E-A-M." He spelled it and smiled. "Dream. Now I like that. That's a birthday gift worth having." He stood straight and gazed down, his eyes a dancing pool of blue. "Dream," he said again, this time with a tone of finality. Chloe felt another rush of warmth. She didn't know why but it was important to her that he liked the gift. Maybe it was because she knew nobody else would care. Chloe placed the key chain back in her bag, "Dream" side up, giving the pocket a slight pat as she pulled the zipper.

"You like it?"

"I like it very much," he said, with a tone so serious in nature that Chloe looked quizzically into his eyes. They were more gold than blue now and she sniffed the air, her eyes widening in amazement. A powerful odor of vanilla filled her nose.

"And tell me, Chloe," he said, his voice soft, steady, a song more than sentence, his fingers pressing gently her arm, "what is it you dream?"

Chloe sniffed hard, turning her head this way and that, trying to discern its source. But it was like searching for the beginning thread of a breeze. Frustrated, she crinkled her nose and looked to his face.

"What do I dream of?" Nobody ever asked her that question and Chloe searched his face for signs of mocking. She hesitated, breathing in deeply the delicious aroma, then letting out a long sigh and biting softly her bottom lip.

"Okay," she said, barely above a whisper. "I'll tell you but you have to promise not to laugh."

For an answer, he squeezed lightly on her arm again. Chloe had never seen a more serious expression than what he wore at that moment. She felt the words bubble in her throat and she rushed to release them.

"I want to be a math teacher just like Mrs. Hamptree, only even better." Chloe clamped her lips tight. Had she really said that out loud? For a second, she felt guilty, partly for suggesting Mrs. Hamptree wasn't the best, partly for suggesting she could be better than Mrs. Hamptree. But an odd warmth coursed through her body and she hugged herself tightly, giggling at the vision of drawing numbers on a board as a roomful of young students gazed in rapt attention. She jumped at the sudden touch on her shoulder.

"That is a fine dream. And it will come true. I'm sure of it." Chloe smiled broadly at his confident tone. For one happy golden moment, she actually believed. Then the cold bit her nose and she shivered.

"Well, I think it's time we moved along again," he said, pulling lightly at her hand, his tone all business again. "Your mother will start to worry."

Chloe dropped her head and kicked at a stone.

"She won't worry," she said flatly. "She'll just get mad."

The man squeezed her hand but said nothing, and for a bit, the two walked in silence, listening to the thud of raindrops against the umbrella and the squish of their shoes on slush.

"One, two, three, four . . ." The thud of raindrops against the umbrella turned rhythmic and Chloe, lost in thought, ticked off a whispered count.

"Five, six, seven, eight—"

"Nine, ten, eleven, twelve," he jumped in, startling Chloe, who didn't know she was speaking loudly enough for him to hear. Before she had time to even feel embarrassed, though, he turned abruptly to his right and stopped short. Clicking his heels together ceremoniously, he shot her a wide, playful smile.

"About-face, young lady," he said, waving his arms grandly as if presenting a marvelous treasure. "We have arrived."

Chloe looked with far less enthusiasm in the direction of his wave. For the first time, she saw her home through the eyes of a stranger. And what she saw brought red to her cheeks.

Before them stood a small, yellow, one-story house, dingy with the kind of smeared overcoat dirt that comes from several years' worth of accumulation. A shoulder-high pile of broken metal shelves and white plastic milk crates was leaned precariously along the walls of the right side of the structure, alongside which stood a girl's bike with a long seat the color of pink; at least, it used to be pink. The sun and rain had done their damage and the color was faded so much that given the right angle, the seat looked more white than pink. Chloe gazed with sadness at the rust of the rims that held flat, lifeless tires, remembering the many times her father promised to fill them with air. The broken bike had become just another mocking symbol of broken promises, broken dreams.

She swept her eyes to the nearby shed with its shamble of roof and broken door, behind which she knew was that night's stash of beer. Hardly an evening passed when her father was home that he didn't sit with his friends on the board placed atop two milkcrates and chug beer after beer, their laughter growing louder with each fresh can. She could see them through her bedroom window, tossing their cans over their shoulders through the broken window of the shed, arguing with each other about who would go inside and get the next round of beer. As the evening wore on, as the drinking game grew more boisterous, their accuracy waned and their cans, rather than whisking through the window and disappearing into dark corners of the shed, began clattering against the siding and spilling to the ground.

It wasn't uncommon for Chloe to count six, seven, eight, or more cans on the ground by the shed as she headed to school in the morning. Curiously, they'd always be gone by the time she arrived home. It was only a guess, but Chloe figured her mother had a hand in making her father clean the mess. Her mother's temper was no match for her father's hangovers.

Chloe smiled ruefully at the thought, as she stole a glance at her companion.

"You are home," he said, gazing with soft eyes into hers.

Perhaps it was his kind look; perhaps it was the unusualness of the walk; or perhaps it was the shame she felt as she surveyed the grim property she called home. Whatever the reason, Chloe's throat tightened and she choked on sudden tears.

She bit her lip hard and squeezed her new friend's hand. He squeezed back just as hard and Chloe sighed, looking one last time onto his face. His eyes were gold and green and an image of a beautiful open field flashed across Chloe's mind, so vivid she could almost smell grass. Then it was gone and it was all cracked cement leading to a dirty front porch, and Chloe sighed again.

"I think this will be the most wonderful birthday you've ever had," the man said, reaching into his pocket and pulling forth a small card, about the size of a business card, and handing it to Chloe. She glanced at it but didn't reach for it.

"Why?" She puzzled at his gentle smile. "Why would you say that?"

"Because you are greatly loved." He handed her the card once again and this time she took it. Against a pattern of red roses wafted the words, in white block letters, "GOD LOVES YOU." Chloe stared, reading the words over and over.

"And now you know it," he said, patting her gently on her knit-capped head.

Chloe stood silent, trying to make out its meaning. She had heard of God, of course, but He meant nothing to her. He was the name of something some people prayed to— not her family, but some people. And for the life of her, she didn't know why people prayed, or what they said during prayers, or why they would speak or whisper to thin air, as if expecting an answer.

But she didn't want to be rude.

"Thanks," she said, forcing a smile while sliding the card into her coat pocket. "Thank you." She stood somewhat awkwardly, knowing she had to go inside but not wanting to say goodbye. Inviting him in was out the question, she knew. But she wondered if she'd ever see him again, and if so, how and when. It dawned on her she didn't even know his name and with a start, she pulled at his hand, which was still safely tucked within her fingers.

"I forgot to get your name. What's your name?"

He flashed another one of his wide smiles and bent slightly while waving his hand theatrically.

"You may call me Mr. Xander—at your service." He gave another grand wave, then bowed.

"Zander?" She said the name to herself several times, before finally nodding and looking up at him.

"With an 'X,'" he said. Chloe scrunched her nose in confusion.

"X-a-n-d-e-r." He smiled again. "X marks the spot, right?"

Chloe considered for a moment, then nodded in approval.

"I like it," she said. "I like it very much." For some reason she couldn't fathom, the name seemed to fit him.

He smiled, then beckoned at the streetlamp they were passing.

The winter sky, still cloudy from the earlier rainfall, had grown even darker, tripping the automatic timer on the lamp, which now poured forth a soggy yellow glow.

"It's funny how time flies, isn't it, Chloe?"

"Oh my gosh!" Chloe pulled her hand from his in panic. "I have to get inside. Now. I have to go." She turned as if to run to the house, then stopped, looked back and took one more glance at his eyes. They were blue again, the same icy blue like when they first met. She felt the same warmth flow through her body from when she first gazed into them and for a brief moment, imagined the whiff of vanilla. But when she sniffed, it was gone. Impulsively, she wrapped her arms around him tight.

"I'll miss you," is all she said, then broke free and raced to the steps. With a hand on the doorknob, she turned for one last look. He was gone. The street was empty and she could see for what seemed like miles in each direction, but he was nowhere to be found. She reached into her coat pocket and felt the hard side of a small stiff card. Sighing, she turned the doorknob and stepped across the threshold into her home. Mr. Xander was right about one thing. In all her nine years of living, this was the best birthday ever. Never before had she received two gifts on the same day.

Chloe carefully let the door shut behind her, hoping the squeak of the metal on the hinge of the screen wouldn't announce her presence—or worse, wake someone. Unfortunately, in her rush to beat the cold, she didn't think about her broken backpack, and it was at that particular moment—with one booted foot inside the door, the other mid-air, moving forward—the already frayed cloth strained just a bit more and snapped.

With first a whack and then a crash, Chloe's bag swung swiftly toward the door, smacking into metal and throwing her off balance. Then came a second crash as the backpack spun forward, striking a vase on the small entryway table and sending it hurtling to the bare floor.

Chloe stood stork still, her frightened body frozen, her ears peeled for the call she knew was coming.

"Chloe!"

She had to answer. She knew she had to answer. But the lump in her throat wouldn't let her utter a word.

"Yes?" she finally squeaked, swallowing hard.

"Chloe!" This time, the voice was even louder, and with a shake of desperation and fear, Chloe wrested herself from her stupor and sprang into action. Scooping as much glass as she could into her hands, she hurried into the kitchen to dump it into the trash, calling as she did, "Coming." She hoped her voice sounded calm, cheerful even. A slight sting on her finger gave her pause and she glanced down, only to see a tiny line of red at the base of her pinkie, where it met the palm. As she watched, the line grew longer and thicker.

"I'm coming!" Chloe said again, wiping her hand on her pants and hustling down the hallway. Instinctively, she dropped her backpack along the way. The fewer triggers she gave her mother to work with, the better. The backpack would be a clue she just arrived home and she didn't need her mother to immediately jump on that.

"Hi, Mom," Chloe said, her tone guarded, her hands pushing gently at the bedroom door. A clink sounded and she looked down, just in time to see a brown beer bottle ricochet off the door and skate across the bare floor. She followed its path with downcast eyes until it settled softly against a brown-stained purse dumped carelessly by the nightstand. She felt her mother's glare and dragged her eyes onto the bed. Chloe tried to keep her face neutral but the sour smell of the room was pulling uncomfortably at her nostrils and she stifled the urge to slide her hand over her face. To do so, she knew, would be a grave mistake.

"What was that sound? Did you break something?"

"Umm." Chloe nervously kicked the toe of her right foot into the heel of her left foot, feeling the gentle bounce as her boot struck the rubber beneath her ankle.

CHLOE

One, two, three, four . . .

With each bounce, she counted, and with each count, she held her breath a bit longer.

"I asked you a question, Chloe!"

Chloe sucked in deep and let go a breath. She didn't dare speak. But she didn't dare stay silent too long either. Her mind raced. Was this a test, to see if she would admit breaking a vase her mother already knew she broke? Chloe bit the inside of her cheek hard, tasting blood with the tip of her tongue as she weighed out how best to answer. Maybe her mother was just angry about something that happened at work, and the sound of the breaking vase woke her, but not enough so she could assuredly know something was broken.

Chloe counted off the possibilities, gazing hard at her mother's face for clues. Then she feared her mother might mistake the stare for a challenge, so quickly she turned her attention to the heaped ashtray on the bedside table. The odor was overpowering. For a second, Chloe's mind drifted to Mr. Xander and the smell of vanilla, and she caught herself before her lips turned upward.

Her mother flung the covers off her body and slowly rose to a sitting position. With the precision that comes from years of practice, she smoothly swung her legs to the floor while reaching hard for her cigarette box. A deft flick, a flash of flame, and a moment later, swirls of smoke blew from her pursed lips. She sighed loudly, so loud it was more groan, and fixed Chloe with a look of reproach.

Her hair was matted and messy, half of it balled and twisted with a black elastic, the other half falling across a pale cheek. Too-bright pink lips pursed tightly around her cigarette, and she pulled hard on her blue smock top to adjust it over her potted belly. One sock dangled, hiding toes painted some time ago a garish purple; the other foot, revealing chipped purple gloss, was bare. She turned her head left, right, and left again, huffing her annoyance with each effort.

Finally, she found what she sought on the floor in front of her and with a grunt, she heaved forward and grasped a can emblazoned with red and blue lettering. With a loud pop, she opened the can and sucked long and noisily. Chloe watched as her cigarette ashes dribbled onto the sheet. Her mother shifted her leg and like that, the ashes disappeared, just another smear among untold numbers of smears on the bedsheet. For the life of her, Chloe couldn't recall her mother ever doing laundry.

Her mother gulped, stifling what would have been a very loud burp, then slowly moved her blurry, bloodshot eyes toward Chloe.

"Come here," she said, pulling at the last of her cigarette and stamping it into the ashtray, sending several butts flying onto the table. She grabbed her pack and stuck another between dry lips. Chloe moved slowly forward, sidestepping a trail of clothing that went from the wall into the middle of the floor. She stopped several feet from her mother.

"I said c'mere!"

Chloe took another step, then another.

"I said get over here!" Her mother lunged and grabbed Chloe by the arm, yanking her hard. "Now what was that sound? What did you break!"

Chloe's heart pumped hard and she swallowed, trying to find her voice.

"I—I—" She struggled to stop stammering.

"I, I, I." Her mother sneered and tossed her cigarette into the ashtray to grab at her with both arms. She jerked Chloe back and forth, as if shaking would somehow free the words from her lips. "What are you, an idiot? You forget how to speak?" She reached up with her right hand and smacked Chloe on the side of the head.

"Maybe that'll shake something loose," she said, giving another shake and smack. She grabbed tight at Chloe's shoulders and held her a foot from her face. Chloe squirmed as her mother's fingers dug deep.

"Stop pulling!" Chloe's mom gave another whack to her head. "Now I asked you a question and I better get an answer this time, or else."

Her mother's breath was rancid, but Chloe didn't dare turn her head. Her mother, grasping both arms again, leaned closer and stared with black eyes.

"Well?"

Breathing in sour, holding back a gag, Chloe whispered, "I broke the vase."

"My vase! My antique vase!" It wasn't a question, but Chloe felt compelled to nod.

She ducked, but not in time. Her mother's blows struck once, twice, three times and Chloe tried in vain to cover her head. Her self-defense only seemed to infuriate her mother further, and she struggled to keep her footing as the blows continued, to her head, her arms, her side, her cheek. Chloe's head grew numb, partly from the slaps, partly from the torrent of vulgar names her mother screamed in her ears. She finally pulled away, tears stinging her cheeks where her mother's handprint burned.

"I'm sorry! I'm sorry! I'm sorry!" Chloe backed away, her head down, trying her best to avoid her mother's hands. "I'll fix it! I'll buy a new one! I'll give you all the money I have to get a new one! I promise!"

Her mother snorted, a mocking, sarcastic, ugly laugh.

"Your money! Your money, huh? What money do you have?" Her eyes narrowed as she stared at Chloe and reached for her cigarette pack. Chloe quickly backed up a couple more steps and raised her head. Shame flooded through her as she wiped quickly at her tears. *I hate you!* she screamed in her mind. But she fought to keep her face neutral, knowing her expression was being graded for disrespect.

"My birthday money from Aunt Masey," she said, as evenly as possible, backing up another step and gulping deep to control her breathing. It wouldn't take much to set her mother off again. Sometimes, even a look of sullen resentment could do it, and in the seconds her mother took to reach for and light another cigarette, Chloe quickly wiped her eyes. She sniffed, then swallowed hard. She felt her mother's angry gaze back on her, but kept her eyes trained on the pattern of the bedspread, counting blue circles and tracing tiny dots in her mind, desperately distracting herself from the stubborn tears that kept pooling, poised to drop. One blink, she knew, and it'd be all over. The last thing she wanted was to give her mother that satisfaction.

One, two, three, four, five. Chloe counted first the circles, then the dots around the circles. *Six, seven, eight, nine, ten.* As soon as she finished one set, she moved on to the next. *One, two, three, four.* As soon as she finished all the sets she could see, she started counting them again. *One, two, three.*

Her mother blew out smoke and regarded her coolly.

"Okay," she said finally, blowing out another billow and fumbling on the floor for something. She pulled her handbag from beneath the bed and plopped it on her lap. Chloe stopped counting for a moment and watched as her mother searched noisily through her bag.

"Okay," she said again, plucking out a small, folded piece of paper and unrolling it on the nightstand. "You can buy a new vase with your freaking birthday money." Chloe watched as her mother pulled forth a dollar bill and rolled it tight, lowered it to the piece of paper and sucked something deep into first one nostril, then another. She wiped her nose and glanced at Chloe.

"This is your fault. You gave me a huge headache. Thanks so much for that," she said sarcastically, pointing a powdery dollar bill in Chloe's direction. "Now go get my money and clean up the mess you made. There better not be one piece of glass on the floor. Not. One. Or else."

The threat hung unstated, but Chloe knew better than to ask. She turned and fled, tears welling again as she caught the final parting name-calls her mother shot her way.

Chloe closed the door as gently as she could, cutting off any more words. She raised her palm and struck angrily at her tears, cursing herself for her weakness. She grabbed her backpack from the hallway and hugged it hard.

Stupid, stupid, stupid, stupid, she told herself, biting her bottom lip until it bled. Why couldn't she ever stop crying? She raced as quietly as she could to her room and threw herself onto her bed. The metal frame squeaked loudly and for a second, she imagined her mother's furious face poking into the doorway. Then she couldn't hold out any longer and she burrowed her face tight into her pillow, smashing her nose flat until she felt pain.

I hate her, I hate her, I hate her, Chloe screamed to herself.

She clenched her fists tight and grabbed hard at her bedspread, wiping first one cheek then the other until her pillowcase was wet and uncomfortable. Why couldn't she keep herself from crying? Why did her mother always beat her that way? Chloe imagined a day when she would stand expressionless before her mother's tirades, letting the words and slaps bounce harmlessly to the floor, staring with unseeing and blank eyes—untouchable, unreachable.

She pictured the look of surprise her mother would give when blow after wretched blow failed to bring neither tears nor cries of fear, or even an acknowledgment. With another sob of frustration and fury, Chloe buried her head deep. It would be a long time, she knew, before she reached that level of control.

Finally, she sat up and let the dull spread through her body. Another day, another fight, another cry. Why should today be any different?

Then she remembered that today had actually been a little bit different, and with a quick "oh!" she reached for her bag. She caught her image in the mirror above her bureau.

Gross, she thought, forgetting for the moment the bag as she took in her disheveled hair, the blotchy skin, the red-rimmed and bloodshot eyes. *You're so ugly. No wonder nobody loves you. No wonder nobody wants to be around you. No wonder everybody hates you.* The dullness of a moment ago turned to disgust then wrath and with a violent flick of her wrist, she ripped open the zipper on her bag and pulled out the silver keychain Mrs. Hamptree had given her. *You're such an ugly, stupid dog*, she thought, glancing again at the mirror as she mouthed the words to herself, and running her thumbnail along the five letters that now seemed so mocking: D, R, E, A, M. She held it between thumb and forefinger, watching the light from her ceiling play off its glitter and counting its gentle spins.

One, stupid, two, stupid, three, stupid, four, stupid.

Dream, stupid.

With a quick motion, she tossed the key chain to the floor and stomped it hard. She moved her foot and stared with grim satisfaction at the flattened metal. Reaching into her pocket, she then pulled forth the card from Mr. Xander.

"God loves you," she said, whispering it, then muttering it, then finally cursing it.

She ripped the card into tiny pieces, and watched as they floated to the floor, a bit of red here, a speck of white there. She sat for several moments, maybe even minutes, staring at the small pile of paper, waiting for the dullness to return to her body—welcoming the dullness when it came.

Slowly, she stretched across her bed, laying the back of her head in the middle of her pillow and grasping her fingers deliberately behind her head. She stared hard at the ceiling, counting seconds between breaths as she imagined the faces of the day; first, Mr. Xander, then her mother, then her teacher, then her mother again. She tried to picture her teacher's reaction at the crushed keychain, and Mr. Xander's expression at the ripped card, and sniffed with satisfaction when she discovered she felt nothing but the slightest stab of guilt, so small it came and went in one heavy exhalation.

"Who the freak is God anyway?" she said to the ceiling. But the ceiling gave no answer.

CHAPTER TWO

"I dare you."

The words were music to Chloe's ears, and she smiled and nodded.

"Okay," Chloe said. "What'll you give?"

Chloe looked at the grinning face of her best friend, Missy, and waited. Last time, it was $5. Time before that, it was a McDonald's milkshake. She was determined to get something even better now.

"Whatdya want?"

Chloe paused, then pointed to her friend's neck.

"I'll take that," she said, nodding at the turquoise and silver chain tucked slightly in the folds of Missy's shirt.

Missy's hand flew to her chest.

"No, not this. Come on. Brad gave me that for my birthday. He'll kill me."

"Tell him you lost it." Chloe shrugged. "It's not like you haven't lost stuff he gave you before."

"That's exactly why I can't tell him that," Missy said, letting out a groan. "He gave me a silver pinkie ring for our one-month anniversary—and I lost that. He gave me those concert tickets for our six-month anniversary—and I lost one of 'em. Still don't know what happened there. At least I found the ring. But now he gives me this necklace for my

23

birthday, and you want me to act like I lost it too? He'll freaking kill me."

"Oh come on. You guys have been going out what, almost a year? If he hasn't killed you by now, he's not gonna kill you over a necklace." Chloe reached for the roach clip and gingerly held the tip to her lips. She drew in deeply and held her breath. She nodded approvingly and pointed at the joint. "Good stuff this time."

Missy took it, and with three quick tokes, finished the remainder. She choked lightly as she flicked away ash and put the clip in her pocket. She let loose a burst of smoke and laughed loudly.

"Yeah it is. But let's not change the subject." She butted Chloe with her shoulder. "It's easy for you to joke about Brad. You don't have a boyfriend. You don't have to worry about getting gifts from guys." She ducked just in time to keep Chloe's hand from smacking the side of her face. They both stumbled with laughter, letting the marijuana have its effect as they made their way from the parking lot to the inside of the mall. They plopped on the first bench they found, and for several minutes, they watched the shoppers, loudly mocking one for her ugly orange sweater vest; snickering mercilessly at another for fat rolls peeking from beneath her too-tight top. They finally stopped when they noticed people staring.

"You think they know?" Chloe asked conspiratorially, nudging Missy with her elbow and watching with trepidation as a security guard seemingly eyed them with suspicion. Missy cleared her throat and lowered her head.

"Be cool," she said.

The security guard's presence sobered them and they sat quietly for a time, gazing mindlessly until he disappeared from view.

"And no, we haven't gone out for a year," Missy said, picking up where they left off a few minutes ago. "Nine months. Well, nine months, almost. In a week it'll be nine months."

"A week! See? You won't have to wait long at all for him to buy you a new necklace," Chloe said, laughing. "Come on, fork it over. You know the rules."

Missy sighed. She pulled the chain from her shirt and gazed at its silvery gleam.

"But I really like this. I like it a lot." She looked at Chloe with widened eyes. "Can't you pick anything else—anything else, at all?"

"Don't try to puppy dog me," Chloe said. "You can put your eyes back in their sockets now. Look, if you didn't want to play today, why'd you start it in the first place?"

Missy sighed again and reached back to unhook the chain from her neck. She dropped it into Chloe's outstretched palm and took a step back, surveying the storefront.

"Fine," she said flatly. "But I want at least five things for this."

"No problem." Chloe smiled confidently and slipped the chain around her neck. "How do I look?"

Missy narrowed her eyes but forced a smile.

"Stupid rules."

The rules of the game were simple. They called it the shopping game but it was actually the stealing game. The one who initiated the dare had to give up whatever the one being dared wanted—else perform the dare herself. And when it came to shoplifting, Chloe, hands down, had Missy beat. In fact, Chloe loved the game so much she couldn't tell if it was more because of the free stuff or because of the thrill of the success. Either way, it was her talent. Chloe couldn't imagine a trip to the mall without stealing something—game or no game.

CHLOE

"All right," Missy said, all businesslike now. "I need a new eyeliner, new mascara, new blush, new lip gloss, and umm, lemme think a minute—oh, I know. A new hair curler."

"A hair curler. Come on, Missy. You know that's like this big." Chloe held up two open palms, facing each other, and pulled them wide about two feet.

"Oh puh-leeze. It's more like this big," Missy said, pushing Chloe's hands closer by almost a foot. "Besides, anyone who can grab jeans off the rack and run, practically right in front of a security guard, can get some makeup and a hair curler. That's like nothing for you."

Chloe paused, chewing the inside of her lip and mulling the many mirrors and cameras in the beauty supply store. But rules were rules.

If she passed up the dare—after Missy already gave her the necklace—she would have to perform the next three dares for free; no reward, no stolen goods, no prize. Chloe learned the hard way it was better to do the dare, no matter how tough the challenge. About a year ago, they had been walking home from a midnight party, so drunk they could barely keep from falling, when they came upon a 7-11 and Missy decided she was hungry. But they didn't have money.

"I dare you," Missy said, laughing, pointing toward the front door. "I dare you to get me some candy bars and donuts. Oh, and another beer."

"No problem," Chloe said, waving her arms majestically while attempting a bow. The move threw her off balance and she fell hard to the pavement. Undeterred, she pulled herself to her feet using her friend's arm as a pole. Gazing at Missy's new sweatshirt, she said, "I'll do it for your U2 sweatshirt."

They stumbled to the entrance, holding each other to keep from falling, when Missy heard the sound of an idling engine and turned to look. Parked at the gas pump was a red sporty coupe, unattended but running. Missy lifted her hand and stretched a long finger toward the store window, where a woman stood at the counter rifling through a pocketbook.

"I change my mind," Missy said, her words badly slurred. "Not hungry now. Tired. Tired of walking. I dare you take the car."

"What? I can't drive. I'm only twelve, stupid." Chloe giggled and grabbed her friend's arm for support.

"No, c'mon, Chloe. C'mon. You can drive. I know you can do it. I dare you. I dare you. That means you hafta do it." Missy hopped a bit and weaved closer to the car. She reached out and slid her hand down the curve of the driver's door. "Come on, come ooooon. Why should we steal a stupid candy bar when we can steal a car? When we can steal a car and go through a drive through?" Missy waved her arms excitedly as the thought formed in her mind. "We can get snacks handed to us right through the window, for cryin' out loud."

She laughed, then hiccupped.

Chloe smacked her on the back.

"Brilliant!" Then her face fell and she turned to face her friend.

"But then how would we pay at the drive-through window? We got no money," Chloe said. "No freaking money at all."

Missy scrunched her face tight, as if considering a great dilemma.

"We'll steal the window!" she finally said, waving her arms again. "And they'll be so scared they'll drop the food."

"That's it!" Chloe reached for the door handle, then stopped and let out a groan of disappointment.

"Heyyy," she said, pulling at Missy's jacket. "Forget it. Here she comes."

They stepped back as the woman pulled open the glass door of the store and walked toward her car. With barely a glance at them, she slid into her front car seat and pulled from the lot.

"Ohh. That wuz a good plan too, Miss."

"Yeah it was. And now you owe me three dares 'cause you didn't get it done."

"Bull!" Chloe started to protest, but was overcome with dizziness. She turned her face toward the ground and vomited.

"That's the rules. That's the rules. Dat's da rules," Missy said, mumbling as she rubbed her hand jerkily on Chloe's back, patting with each heave.

After that, Chloe had to steal, in order, a pair of designer sunglasses, a pair of sterling silver skeleton-shaped earrings, and a set of bangle bracelets for Missy, all without getting anything in return. Every time after that Missy wore her U2 sweatshirt, the memory of that evening rubbed raw. *All that work for nothing*, Chloe thought bitterly. She vowed never again.

"So what's it gonna be?"

Missy's voice cut through her reverie, and Chloe looked from her friend's face to the beauty shop, sizing up the number of shoppers she could see and calculating the difficulty of dodging the cameras.

"All right," Chloe said, pulling Missy to a nearby bench. "Wait here. I'll get your stupid curling iron."

"And the makeup too? Don't forget the makeup."

"Yeah, yeah, I'll get the makeup too," Chloe said. "Sit here, just stay here and I'll be back in a few."

"Hey, make sure it's black eyeliner and black mascara, okay? Don't get any of that gray crap," Missy called after her, waving her arms so wildly she almost knocked the cup from the hand of an elderly woman as she passed. The woman's husband glared at her as he slipped his arm around his wife's shoulder.

"Aww, screw you," Missy muttered, flashing a bony third finger at his back as they passed and plopping into her seat on the bench.

The mall wasn't especially crowded but the store was, and Chloe stood outside its doorway for several seconds, sweeping her eyes toward the ceiling corners to count cameras. It was the ones she couldn't see that were more the problem. The office door had a mirror where the glass was supposed to go and Chloe imagined security guards zeroing in on her as she entered, watching her every move.

It helped her stay on her game if she imagined the worst.

Casually, she reached out and grabbed a pair of earrings off the display, holding them up to her lobes and preening before the small mirror mounted on the wall. She glanced in its reflection for any signs of salesgirls then feigned disgust with the earrings and hung them gently back in their place. With a fingertip, she touched a pair here, a pair there, removing one more to inspect the price tag on the back. After holding it a bit, she put it back with seeming reluctance.

Stealing, to Chloe, was very much like a stage drama. It was the little movements that mattered most—the slight scrunch of the nose, as if pondering the purchase, or the hard gazes between two items, comparing which might work best when brought home. Sometimes, she invented such lively backstories in her mind about the objects of her intended thefts that she forgot she was there to steal. She got swept into her own imaginations of which necklace matched best the dress in her closet, or what scarf would drape most naturally around the collar of her coat. It was all good. The more absorbed with the theatrics, the easier the act.

She smiled, working the cameras she knew were watching.

She had established herself as someone who could take small items off shelves and return them—a trusted shopper.

With a small shake of the head, she wandered down the aisles and toward the makeup section, her fingers loosely cupped around a pair of silver-toned earrings she concealed within her hand.

Her eyes glanced across the eyeliner displays first. Mentally, she discounted the ones in cardboard packaging. They were larger and often contained hidden theft control devices. She moved toward a glass jar containing loose single eyeliner sticks and pulled one from the pack. With a smooth, quick slide of her fingers, she slipped it, along with the earrings, up the left cuff of her jacket, at the same time reaching for a mascara with her right hand. Then she reached with her left hand and took another mascara package off the display, pretending to compare the two. She stared into the distance, her head slightly tilted, then suddenly jerked, letting her lips form a small circle as she noticed the very item she almost forgot she wanted to buy, and she reached for it. Expertly, she slipped a mascara into her cuff once again and with the other hand, brought the pale pinkish blush she had just grabbed off the shelf toward her eyes for closer scrutiny.

Yes, this was just what she needed, she decided, slapping the blush case against her palm and walking back to the mascara section to return the one still in her hand to its position on the shelf.

Three down. Two to go. She smiled slightly as she wiped at her forehead, glancing at the pretend sweat on her fingertip before brushing the hand that still held the container of blush against her side. She really did love to shop.

She wiped her forehead once more then pulled up her jacket until the waistband was snug across her stomach. Slowly, she lowered the zipper, exhaling a bit as she fanned the cloth of her coat against her body. She was a shopper who was beginning to get hot, nothing more, and she smiled brightly at the woman walking toward her. As they passed, Chloe shifted slightly and with a single quick movement, dropped the blush into the side of her jacket, in the space between her underarm and the waistband. She searched the shelves for the hair curler section.

"Can I help you find anything?"

The salesgirl's voice startled Chloe, and for a second her heart froze. Then she flashed a smile. The girl looked young, a high-schooler working part-time for college money.

"No, I'm good."

"Okay, let me know if I can help you find anything."

Chloe watched her walk away, letting her breathing go back to normal. *One more,* she thought, swallowing hard as she glanced at the other shoppers. With relief, she saw the aisle with the curling irons was somewhat crowded. The more customers, the easier to hide from the cameras. Chloe slipped in between a woman and a teenage girl who were standing near the curling irons, and immediately looked for the smallest box of the bunch. She gently touched the side of her jacket where the blush container was concealed, making sure it hadn't slipped from its spot. Satisfied it wasn't going to pop forth when she reached out with her arms, Chloe carefully lifted a curling iron from the shelf, then another. With a glance to the left then the right, she dropped one to the floor and while bending to retrieve, stuffed the other beneath her coat. Standing straight, she zipped her coat and put the iron back where it belonged.

Time to go. She turned and walked quickly to the exit, keeping her eyes fixed straight ahead while she counted steps.

Three, four, five. Just a few more feet. Seven, eight, nine.

"Miss?" Chloe felt a chill run through her body. She kept walking. *Fifteen, sixteen, seventeen.*

"Miss, could you please stop for a moment? I'd like to talk to you."

The voice was authoritative and masculine. For a second, Chloe considered running. But the doorway was blocked by a woman with a baby carriage. She gulped and turned, forcing her face into an expression of surprise and annoyance.

"What?" Chloe swallowed hard at the dark eyes peering with open suspicion at her.

"Could you come with me, please?"

Chloe looked toward the bench where Missy was waiting, watching, with wide eyes and open mouth.

"For what?" Chloe fought to stay in act, feigning the sharp tone of a shopper needlessly halted.

"Just come with me, please."

Silently, Chloe obeyed. She followed him past the rows of shelves, at first keeping her head lowered to avoid the curious glances of customers, but then deciding it would be better to look them in the eyes. Innocent people, after all, had nothing to hide. And since she didn't know what he knew, her best course of action was nonchalance. *Nothing to see here; just getting the officer's help finding some missing keys, that's all.*

He stepped back and beckoned her to pass.

"Go ahead." He held open the door to an office that Chloe, minutes earlier, hadn't known existed. Her heart fell as she surveyed the dozen or so screens mounted on the walls, each one displaying a section of the store. She sucked in her breath as she saw a closeup of the shelf containing the curling irons and instinctively, she felt at her side. The box was still there. Her body grew hot beneath her coat and she began to sweat for real.

Her parents thought she was at the library, studying for a test with a classmate. If they found out the truth, she would be grounded, confined to the house for at least a week, maybe two. Chloe glanced at the face of the security officer, but his grim expression made her heart sink lower. She was fairly certain he wasn't going to let her leave without at least placing a telephone call to her parents.

"Have a seat," he said, nodding at the chair he pulled for her, before plopping his body in his own and swiveling the seat to face her. He scooted forward until he was closer than he needed to be, and then he sat motionless and gazed at her, for several silent moments.

Chloe fought the urge to nibble at the corner of her bottom lip.

"Suppose you tell me what you have inside your jacket," he finally said.

"What?" She pursed her lips as if he had asked the preposterous.

"Look." He tapped at the television screen on the desk, then beckoned with a wave of his finger at the others mounted on the wall. "Look around you. See all those security monitors and cameras? We can do this the easy way or we can do this the hard way." He let his words sink in, then continued.

"Suppose you just open your jacket and let me see what you've got there and then I can tell the police how you cooperated and how they should go easy on you. Makes everybody's lives easier, even yours."

Chloe crossed her arms over her chest and fixed him with a stony stare.

"I don't know what you're talking about."

His glares didn't frighten Chloe. Her parents had long ago taught her there were much worse things than dirty looks. What did give her pause, though, was his abrupt reach for the telephone and the picture of her father's enraged face flashing across her mind.

"I'll just let the police deal with this then," he said, beginning to dial. He paused. "What's your name?"

Chloe chewed her lip but said nothing.

"Come on now," he said, his tone growing impatient. "It's like this: I can call the police first, and we can sit here and wait for the police to come—they can take twenty minutes, they can take two hours, it just depends on how busy they are. And then, as soon as the cops get here, they're going to say I need to call your parents and get them down here because you're a juvenile and they can't question you without one of your parents present. So then we'll either have to wait even longer for your parents to get here, or— and this is probably what'll happen—the police will arrest you, cuff you, walk you through the mall to their car, so everybody in the mall will get a good look at you, and then take you to the station and sit you on a bench or stick you in a locked room until you decide to give up your name and your phone number so they can call your parents to the police station."

He paused to check what effect his words were having.

"Or," he said, tilting his head and sighing, "you can just give me your name now, and then a phone number where I can reach your parents, or your mom or dad or whoever takes care of you, and I can call them first."

Chloe fought the urge to cry. She wasn't positive he was telling the truth, but what he described seemed about right, and in the end, it almost didn't matter. All roads led to her parents. She wished fervently for the floor to open and swallow her whole.

"Like I said, we can do this the easy way or the hard way."

She stared hard at the floor once more, but it was futile.

"Chloe Richards," she said quietly.

"And your phone number?" He punched in each digit as she spoke. "Hello, Mr. Richards?"

Chloe's heart thumped so hard she thought he could hear it. Her mom would've been tough enough. But her dad—her dad! She cursed her luck. He wasn't ever home at this hour. He wasn't ever home at most hours, really. His cross-country trucker job kept him on the road more days of the year than not. When he was home, he was drunk, or on his way to being drunk, or on his way back from being drunk. It was the third possibility Chloe most feared. That was when he was the most unpredictable.

"He'll be here in fifteen minutes."

Chloe hugged her chest tight, feeling the hard tip of the curling iron box positioned uncomfortably against her rib cage, reminding her of the trouble to come. The guard, having dispensed with the announcement of her father, and apparently deciding she wasn't going to talk, turned his back and busied himself with clicking on a keyboard at his desk. Chloe watched his arms as they jerked with each stroke, then watched the clock as it ticked down minutes. In growing desperation, she looked for a place to dump the evidence.

To her left was a file cabinet; to her right, an empty trash barrel; to her front, the security guard and his desk. His back was still to her and he was now busily sifting through a pile of papers, but Chloe suspected he was keeping an eye on her just the same. Besides, it was so quiet that she feared even the slightest lowering of her zipper or the tiniest repositioning of her arms would draw his attention. She resigned herself to the fact she was going to get grounded. Her goal now was to keep from getting hit by her father. And if she couldn't keep from getting hit, then her goal was to not get hit too much. She sighed, knowing the next few days weren't going to be pleasant at all.

A buzzer sounded on the desk and the security guard snapped at a button.

"Hey, Joe," the voice at the other end said. "There's a guy here, Shane Richards, says you want to see him?"

"Send him in," Joe said. He turned in his chair to face Chloe and was about to say something when three sharp raps at the door startled them both. They were more thuds than knocks and the security guard named Joe shot to his feet so quickly it reminded Chloe of that military movie she had seen, the part where the drill sergeants ordered around their terrified recruits. She gazed curiously at him for a moment before remembering the knocks were meant for her. She cast her eyes back to the floor and held her breath.

Joe straightened his shoulders, fixed a neutral smile on his face, and reached for the doorknob.

"Mr. Richards? I'm . . ." he said, and his smile disappeared.

Chloe's father was an imposing man in height and weight, fully six foot and hitting 200 pounds, give or take a few six packs. His blondish gray hair hung in unruly knots below the collar of his well-worn plaid flannel, which was covered by an equally well-worn gray hoodie sweatshirt. His faded jeans, fastened sloppily just below his potbelly with a thick brown belt, were stained with flecks of white paint, and his tan work boots were thick and heavy, smeared with grease and more paint. He carried the distinct odor of vinegar or perhaps it was soured apple cider, and cigarette smoke wherever he went.

He glared at Chloe with slitted eyes, unblinking above his bulbous, reddened nose. And as he stood there, his body filling the doorway, she shivered and wished she had just let the police come and take her to the safety of the jail cell.

After what seemed like days, he finally turned toward Joe, his glare just as intense.

"Why didn't you just call the cops and let them take her." It was a statement, not a question.

Joe shuffled his feet uncomfortably and shot Chloe a look of almost compassion.

"Oh, I'm sure that's not necessary," he said, taking a couple steps away from him and laughing nervously. "I mean, I think—I think we could probably handle this in-house, without the police." He cleared his throat several times as he flitted his eyes back and forth from the floor to the wall to Chloe's father, then finally fixed them on the security camera in the far corner, where he stared with all his might in what he hoped gave the appearance of an important work situation requiring immediate attention. After several moments, during which he took several deep breaths, Joe let his eyes wander back to the plaid collar of the figure in the doorway, and said, with as much of an authoritative tone as he could muster, "I've got your daughter on camera taking several items from the store and putting them in her jacket. I need you to ask her to open her jacket and return them to the store."

Chloe's father said nothing. But his silence was more than enough. She felt his waves of anger, even as she kept her head tilted stubbornly at the floor.

Suddenly, he stepped toward her and with one quick movement, yanked down her zipper. The intensity of his action pushed her to the side so hard she nearly fell. Then three pairs of eyes all at the same time turned to look at the box that thudded to the floor. For a moment, time stood still. Chloe was the first to look away. She shot a glance at her father and what she read in his face sent a coldness through her body.

"Thief!" His eyes were darts and Chloe started to shake.

She dug her elbow tight to her side, hoping against hope the container of blush didn't drop as well. But her father reached for her again and instinctively, she stepped back, and when she did, she lifted her arms just enough so that she lost the grip on the blush. It popped out and plopped on the floor. This time, only four eyeballs looked downward; Chloe kept hers fixed on her father as he strode to grab her arm. His fingers cut through the cloth to her shoulder and he dug them in so hard she cried out.

"What else," he said, twisting on her shoulder even tighter. His voice was a hiss and Chloe felt his hot breath against her ear.

Joe cleared his throat and coughed.

"Umm. I think maybe we should all take a minute and calm things down a bit?"

Chloe felt the fingers on her shoulder relax. Her father stepped away and she quickly readjusted her jacket, reaching a careful finger beneath the cuff on her wrist to feel for the other three items. They were still there, securely laying against her skin. She glanced to Joe, but he was looking at her father, a strange expression on his face.

"I think maybe," he said, then he cleared his throat, looked at Chloe, then started again. "I think maybe we could just deal with this without bringing in the police and chalk it up to a youthful indiscretion. How old are you, Chloe?"

"She's twelve," her father answered for her, his voice still angry. "Old enough to know better."

"Has she ever done this before?"

Chloe shook her head hard, then stopped when her father flicked his glance at her.

"She's never been caught. No."

Joe cleared his throat again and slapped his palms together lightly.

"Okay," he said briskly. "Then I think we can handle this ourselves. It's store policy that Chloe will never be allowed to come in here again, and if she does, we will have to immediately call the police. But other than that, and so long as she returns these items—" and he waved lightly at the blush and curling iron box still on the floor—"then I think we can just move on."

The room was silent for a moment. Joe cleared his throat again and took a step toward the door.

"That means you can go home."

Chloe, head down, shuffled toward the door. She hesitated when she got to her father, who hadn't yet moved. Another uncomfortable silence filled the room and for several seconds, neither Chloe nor Joe knew how Chloe's father was going to proceed. Then he reached for the door and flung it wide open, banging it loudly against the wall and catching it before it bounced closed again.

"Go," he said, and Chloe went, ducking her head slightly as she passed before him.

They said nothing as they made their way to the mall exit. Then as soon as their feet hit asphalt, Chloe's father lit into her, so loudly it drew the attention of several shoppers.

"What were you thinking?" He unleashed a string of obscenities so vicious a woman walking past with her toddler reached to cover the boy's ears.

"A thief! I didn't raise you to be a thief." He pulled his car keys from his pocket and clicked open the front passenger door. He grabbed at Chloe's shoulder and slung her into the seat. Chloe rubbed her arm and quickly checked to be sure the makeup items in her sleeve were still concealed as he walked around the truck to his driver's door.

He barely closed the door before she felt the smack of the back of his right hand against her face. Tears welled in her eyes and she fought to keep them from falling.

"You little thief!" He struck her on the cheek again, then again. Chloe tried to duck, but he grabbed at the bottom of her chin and thrust her head against the seat. He slapped twice more before letting go of her face and thrusting his key into the ignition. The truck started with a roar and Chloe turned tear-streaked eyes to the window, watching with shame as a teenage couple passed and stared. She wished fervently he would lower his voice, but he just glared at the couple and shouted louder.

"You belong in jail. You belong in juvie. How do you think I like coming off the road to get a call about you stealing?" He slapped her again. "You're just like your slut mother. You never should've been born."

He reached across her lap to the glovebox and pulled out a small bottle filled with clear liquid. He unscrewed the cap and the smell of alcohol filled the cab. Chloe sniffled as he gulped noisily. When he was done, he threw the bottle at her feet then cursed as he yanked the shifter aggressively into drive.

"Just like your mother, nothing but a cheap whore," he muttered, peeling from the parking lot.

Chloe felt the throb of her shoulder at the spot where her father had twisted and dug in his fingers, but she didn't dare move to rub it; didn't dare even more her head, even though the sharp angle she held it toward her window was causing an ache. She fought the instinct to reach up and rub her neck.

"You know, you brought this on yourself. Don't come crying to me about your arm hurting or your head hurting or whatever other baby hurt you come up with. It's your own fault. Keep your complaints to yourself."

The drive home was short and he spun wheels as they hurtled into the driveway, then slammed on his brakes so quickly he sent Chloe smashing into the glove box. He threw more curses her way as he tore open his door and stormed to her side of the truck.

"Get out," he said, breathing vodka inches from her face. He yanked her jacket and she fell to the ground.

"Get up." He pulled her arm hard, but his slap reeled her back to the ground. She sat in a crumple as he pointed toward the shed.

"See that?" He kicked at her leg until she raised her head and looked. "See all that around there?" He waved his hand vaguely at the pile of beer cans; the bags of trash, some of which had opened and spread their contents on the ground;

the scattered pieces of broken furniture—a lawn chair with ripped and frayed straps, a metal folding chair broken in two; an old loveseat with ripped cushions, one of which had been dropped on the ground and further torn open, its blackened cotton insides spilling forth like a regurgitated meal.

"See all that?" He glared down at her. "And inside—inside there's more. I want you to clean this up. Clean everything up. Get rid of all the garbage. Get rid of everything in the yard and in the shed that doesn't belong there." He slipped his hand inside his jacket pocket and pulled out a beer. Popping the can open, he slugged it back and then, with a red-eyed glare at Chloe, he flung it at her.

"That too," he hiccupped, striding toward the house. "And don't you even try coming inside until it's all done."

Chloe felt the chill of the late afternoon air and bit back the sobs brewing in her chest. The shed, she knew, was piled high with trash bags her parents never took to the dump. When the winds were right, the smell of rotted food would sometimes drift toward her bedroom window. In the summer, she couldn't keep her window open even a little, else the odor of trash would fill her room and cause her to gag.

The idea of having to now touch those same bags revulsed her.

She strained her neck and looked down the street as far as she could see and imagined where the road would lead if she just got up and started walking—if she simply picked herself off the ground and left the yard and kept going and going until she was too tired to go any more. She imagined the look on her father's face as he came to check her progress and saw the bags untouched, the trash still strewn, and then with anger, called to her and searched for her, but she was nowhere to be found.

She pictured him storming to get his belt, the stiff, leather one he kept handy on the hook on the bathroom door, the one he used as a whip on her bottom and legs and back whenever she disobeyed or talked back or, just whenever, and then calling for her, and shouting for her to come. She thought of the expression on his face, the disbelief in his eyes, as he realized she wasn't coming—as he realized she was gone.

She wondered if either of her parents would bother to look for her or call the police, and she doubted it. Sitting on the ground while her legs grew cold and damp from the dirt, she thought for sure they wouldn't care at all if she disappeared. She felt a stab of anger, but not at her parents—at herself. She had nowhere to go and she was too scared to leave. Chloe clenched her fingers tight, digging the nails into the palms of both hands until tiny little dots of red appeared. Then she got up and walked toward the shed, her shoulders drooped low as she counted the number of years until she turned eighteen.

CHAPTER THREE

Chloe felt the light tap on her shoulder and turned with annoyance.

"Hi there. I'm Ellie. I'm from Alabama."

Chloe stared, open-mouthed, at the petite girl in the desk behind her—the girl's hair piled high in a bun. It was the first time she had ever heard a deep Southern accent. It could've been French, for all it mattered, or German.

"What'd you say?" Chloe asked rudely.

"I'm Ellie. I just moved here."

Chloe stared again. Finally, her eyes blank, she muttered, "Congratulations," and turned back to the paper on her desk, marked at the top with a blaring red, "F." A face from another time, her grade-school math teacher, Mrs. Hamptree, flashed through her mind and for a moment, Chloe felt regret. Then she pursed her lips and shrugged, crumpling the paper until it was a tight little ball, then shoving it into the pocket of her backpack under her chair.

Math sucks, she thought, pulling out a piece of gum from her pocket and popping it into her mouth. The annoying tapping on her shoulder started again and she turned with a grunt.

"What!" Chloe watched with satisfaction as Ellie drew back sharply against her chair.

"I just," Ellie said, searching for the right words, "I mean, I just thought you might want to be partners for the project?"

Her question trailed into a whisper and Chloe squinted her face in confusion.

"What?"

Ellie leaned forward and smiled.

"I just thought you might want to be partners for the project?"

Chloe gave her a look of scorn and was just about to shake her head when the teacher spoke.

"Your partner will be the person sitting behind you—unless, of course, you're sitting in the last row, in which case your partner will be the person sitting in front of you." The teacher gave a quick laugh, then started slapping stacks of stapled paper on each desk. "You have five minutes to rearrange your desks so you're partnered off, facing your partner. Then I want you and your partner to spend the rest of the class time going through the first two sections and answering the questions. I want to know your topic before the end of class." She tossed a packet on Chloe's desk and added somewhat ominously, "You will not leave this room until you and your partner have told me your topic."

Chloe sighed loudly and with a sharp turn of her body, pivoted her desk so it faced Ellie's. She was just about to say something very unkind about Ellie's broad smile when she saw from the corner of her eye the teacher walking up a nearby row and thought better of it. She settled for a grimace instead, followed by another long sigh as Ellie failed to take note.

"This is going to be fun. I just know we're going to be the best of partners," Ellie whispered, her strange accent ringing in Chloe's ears. "You know, you're on my bus. You sit in the back and pass me every day. I sit more toward the front. I see you get dropped off, though. You live in that yellow house set back from the road, don't you? I live a couple stops away. We don't live that far from each other. We could probably get together after school for this project at my house. Or yours."

Chloe bit her tongue, holding back another snarky comment.

Ellie, meanwhile, kept up a steady stream of happy chatter as she flipped through the pages, pointing at the drawings and reading out loud the printed directions. Chloe withstood it as long as she could, then dramatically pushed her chair back and stood.

"I'll be back. I have to go to the bathroom," she said flatly, ignoring Ellie's surprised look. She reached into her backpack and with a quick turn of her head toward the teacher, pulled something into her pocket. She stuffed her hand on top of it and kept it there while calling out to the teacher.

"May I be excused, Mrs. Wall?"

Chloe took the hall pass Mrs. Wall wrote for her and hurried from the room. She let the door slam behind her and walked quickly to the bathroom on the bottom floor, passing two others in the process. She checked the stalls for feet and, finding none, entered the last one, farthest from the door. Standing on the toilet seat, she reached up and turned the metal crank opening the small glass window near the top of the wall. Then she pulled from her pocket a plastic sandwich bag rolled into a tight little ball. Carefully, so as not to spill the contents, she unrolled the bag and removed a half-smoked joint, a lighter, and a tiny blue pill. She swallowed the pill dry while flicking her lighter, then took a couple of deep drags and held the smoke in her chest until it burned. Coughing, she blew it as best she could to the window. Most drifted outside, and she fanned madly at the few wisps that hovered in her stall.

She finished smoking and rubbed the paper between her finger and thumb, squashing any lit embers before dropping the tiny leftovers into the toilet and flushing.

She hated math.

She especially hated how her math teachers refused to leave her alone each semester she failed math, and instead pushed her to buckle down and try harder. It's like they couldn't get it through their heads that those days of competing in school math contests and winning at the regional and national levels were over for Chloe and she no longer cared about praise for her problem-solving abilities or about recognition for her analytical brilliance. It's like they didn't want to let go of the fact Chloe was done with studying, done with the after-school practice, done with tests and exams and tutorials and special sessions—done with it all. It's like they didn't believe her when she told them she hated math.

She fanned the air some more, smirking at the stupidity of her teachers.

Dimly, through the haze of the drug taking effect in her mind, in her body, she remembered the last time she liked math. It was eighth grade; she won a trip to compete in Washington, D.C., and the night before, her parents fought through the night, into the early morning hours. Chloe, on the heels of a sleepless night, her nerves rattled and raw from listening and her temper on edge at the thought of having to face a long bus ride and a tough national math competition, made the mistake of sniping at her father as he cracked open yet another beer on the couch.

"Haven't you had enough?"

She barely muttered above a whisper, but he heard. He heard and he tore toward her, grabbing her by the hair and yanking so hard she screamed. He dragged her from the house and tossed her into the snow. No matter how she begged and pleaded to get her backpack, to get her clothes for school, to get a covering for her nightgown, and shoes for her bare feet, the door stayed locked. Chloe spent the day and all that night until the next afternoon hunkered in the shed for warmth, gagging on the odors of rotted trash and animal waste.

When she finally returned to school three days later, her teachers called her into the principal's office and berated her for missing the competition. She was given three days' detention for her irresponsible behavior and another round of scolding for leaving her fellow competing classmates out to dry.

It was shortly after that she started bringing home "Fs" on her math tests.

"Oh, well," she said out loud, jumping off the toilet and giggling as she thought of Ellie. *Poor Ellie, sitting by herself in math class, waiting for her partner to return. Waiting for her new friend to come back*, Chloe thought, with another loud giggle. An idea crept into her head as she washed the smoke from her hands and scrubbed hard with soap.

"Oh, Ellie," she said to herself, peeking down the hallway both ways before stepping out of the bathroom and hurrying back to class. "This will be the first fun math in a long time."

The door thudded shut and Chloe, a bit unsteady, reached to balance herself against the wall as she walked.

"Okay, I'm back," Chloe said, sliding into her chair and flashing Ellie the widest of smiles. She couldn't wait to put her plan into motion. She spun her packet around and was just about to flip the page when she noticed a small grouping of letters in the bottom corner. She leaned in closer to read.

"What the freak is this!" Chloe shot Ellie a look of pure disdain, then tapped hard as she read the words again, this time out loud.

GOD LOVES YOU. Chloe's eye fell on her notebook, in the corner of her desk. GOD LOVES YOU—maybe six, seven times. She stared then lifted her notebook cover.

GOD LOVES YOU.

Chloe glared at Ellie and grabbed a black ink pen from her backpack. With hard, angry strokes, she drew dark lines over every letter, on every page Ellie had written, and when she finished, she went back and drew heavy, tiny circles over the letters she just blotted.

"Why did you do this?" Chloe said, scribbling as she hissed through clenched teeth. She felt a stab of satisfaction as Ellie's eyes widened and showed white.

"I'm—I'm sorry," Ellie finally said. "I didn't think it would get you mad. I just—I just—" Ellie stopped and watched Chloe's furious scribbling and waited.

"I just was being friendly," she finally said, spreading her hands helplessly. "I mean, I wasn't doing anything I thought would get you ticked off. I mean—I mean, God does love you. I wasn't saying anything bad."

Chloe's face turned bright red and she quickly glanced around to see if anyone heard.

"You're a moron, you know that?" she said, turning back to Ellie.

"You're a moron," she said again, shaking her head with disgust. "There is no God. You know that, right?"

Ellie's mouth dropped open and for a second, she looked as if she was struggling to say something. Then she apparently decided better and snapped it shut. She dropped her eyes to her desk, fingering the edges of her packet of papers nervously.

"I'm sorry," she said finally, not looking up. Then she mumbled something else, something Chloe didn't quite catch.

"What'd you say? God what?" Chloe's tone was brusque and Ellie flinched but kept her eyes on the papers before her.

"Nothing. Forget it."

Chloe regarded her silently for a moment, then shrugged and turned to the math packets. *Of all the people I had to get partnered with*, she thought.

"So," Chloe said, flapping the pages loudly and smacking them against the palm of her hand, "do you know which one of these you wanna do?"

Ellie looked up and gave a faint smile.

"Look," she said, rolling her pen through her fingers as she spoke, "I really am sorry. Okay? I didn't mean to offend you. It's just that where I come from, it's no big deal—it's no big deal talking about God, or writing that God loves you. It's kind of what my friends and I always did."

Chloe didn't answer.

"I didn't know you didn't believe in God," Ellie finally said. "I'm sorry."

For some reason, Ellie's accent and the way she said the word "sorry" struck as hilarious to Chloe, and she began to giggle. The more she giggled, the more she tried to control her giggling the less she could. Ellie's shocked face wasn't helping either.

"It's fine," Chloe said finally, catching a glimpse of the teacher and lowering her voice. "Really, it's fine."

Ellie smiled with relief, taking Chloe's laughter as a sign of forgiveness.

"Okay," she said brightly, her Southern accent crackling. She flipped the pages of the packet, pointing to the various project descriptions as she went. "So, do you feel like designing a zoo? Or building a house? We could do the scale construction one of a mansion—or of a baseball field. Or maybe you're more the origami type?" Chloe turned the pages slowly, trying to find the math project that would require the least amount of effort and time. She imagined her weekends stuck at a desk with Ellie and groaned out loud.

A golden image caught Chloe's attention.

"What's this?" She pulled the packet to see it better, glancing at various pictures of the Parthenon alongside a strange symbol of a vertical line flowing into an open circle. "The golden ratio?"

Ellie bobbed her head vigorously, happy to reach agreement.

"That looks interesting. Is that the one you want to do?" Chloe raised her eyebrows at Ellie's excited outburst.

"Take it easy, there," she said, but then smiled, to blunt her scorn. "Okay, yeah. This one works."

Chloe pushed away the packet and yawned. Her stomach growled and she hugged herself tight.

"Hey, you don't happen to have any chocolate, do you? No?" Chloe bit her lip as if considering a serious matter. "How about potato chips? You got any chips in your bag?"

Chloe felt a hand on her shoulder and for a second, froze. Was she busted?

"As much as I'm happy to see you engaging with your partner, I don't think there are any math projects in that packet that have to do with chocolate or potato chips, Chloe," her teacher said, looking down and tapping the packet on her desk. "How about we focus on the assignment instead?"

"Oh, we're done," Ellie said, her voice chirpy. "Chloe picked the Parthenon."

Her teacher nodded approvingly.

"The golden ratio," she said, patting Chloe on the shoulder again before moving on. "Very good."

For a split second, Chloe felt excited, thinking of the research and the mystery of the golden ratio and whether the mathematical concept was part of the building of the Parthenon. She recently read a couple headlines about a reconstruction project at the Parthenon that wiped away any theories of this mathematical concept as the foundation of its initial building, and she was curious to learn more. But then something whispered softly in her mind, *But you hate math*, and like that, she was back in the present. She rolled her packet into a messy little scroll and thrust it into her backpack, making sure to crush it beneath her books.

Watching Ellie place her packet neatly into her folder, slide the folder between a couple of nicely stacked folders in her backpack, and then carefully zip the bag and place it gently on the back of her chair, gave Chloe an idea.

"Hey," she said, leaning forward until she was just inches from Ellie's face. "You wanna go to a party tonight with me?"

Ellie looked surprised. "Really?"

"Yeah, it'll be fun." Chloe giggled and put her hand to her mouth. "Fun, fun, fun." The word struck her as hilarious and she dropped her head to her desk, wrapping her arms around her forehead and pushing tight. She fought to control her laughter.

"So," she said finally, raising her head and wiping imaginary spittle from the corners of her lips, "you wanna go or what?"

"I'll have to ask my mom," Ellie said hesitantly. She paused a second or two, then fiddled uncomfortably with her pencil. "Usually, she only lets me go to parties after she's talked to the parents. Or if she knows them from church. Do you think the parents of whoever's throwing the party might talk to my mom on the phone first?"

Chloe bit her lip hard to keep from bursting out laughing.

Oh, this was too good to be true, she thought.

"Look," Chloe said, turning her desk to face the front of the classroom so Ellie wouldn't see her face contorted in mirth, "I know these people really well. Sandy—it's her birthday party—she's been my friend since middle school. And her parents are strict as anything. They wouldn't let her throw a wild party." Chloe paused for effect, and hoped her lie was convincing. "They even go to church every Sunday too."

Ellie considered for a moment. "So Sandy's parents will be there to supervise?"

Chloe coughed back another laugh.

This girl is too much, she thought.

"Sure." Chloe reached back and gave Ellie's arm a quick pat. "Trust me."

The bell rang and the teacher's last-minute directions drowned out any other questions Ellie may have asked. Chloe hurriedly grabbed her bag and slung it over her shoulder. She didn't want to get stuck walking with Ellie to their next class. At the door, Chloe turned and called back, tapping her foot with impatience as she saw Ellie was nearly packed.

"You said you know where I live, right?"

Ellie looked up and with a rush, scooped her books into her arms and started to walk toward Chloe. The point of her shoe struck the leg of a chair, and she stumbled. Chloe smiled as her books toppled to the floor.

"Just come down to my house about seven. You won't even have to knock," Chloe called, taking advantage of Ellie's mishap and stepping into the hallway. "Gotta go! I'll just meet you in the driveway."

She reached into her backpack and without looking, felt around for the plastic baggie she took to the bathroom an hour earlier. She pulled out the other pill, popped it into her mouth and grabbed a quick drink from the hallway water fountain.

Two more classes, she thought with a smile. She couldn't wait to introduce Ellie to her friends.

"Are you sure her parents are okay with this?" Ellie asked, climbing warily from Chloe's beat-up car, her flowery blue dress blowing lightly in the breeze. She glanced at Chloe's ripped jeans and black jacket. "Are you sure I'm not going to be overdressed?"

"You're fine," Chloe said, ignoring Ellie's first question. "I told you, my friends don't judge." She choked back a chuckle as she watched Ellie take delicate steps across the grass, lifting the hem of her ankle-length dress just enough so the blades didn't touch.

CHLOE

"You'll be perfectly fine," Chloe said again, scanning the row of cars as they walked by and suddenly grabbing Ellie by the arm.

She pointed to a dark blue Ford with shiny new rims and a skeleton figure dangling from the rearview mirror.

"Come on," she said, pulling Ellie toward the house impatiently. "I want you to meet someone really cool."

Even from the driveway, they could hear the piercing screams of an electric guitar and the rhythmic thump of drums belting from a system with the bass setting turned too high. The ground as they mounted the front steps seemed to be shaking in time to the beat. The door was partially open and Chloe pushed right in, dragging Ellie by the shoulder of her dress.

The living room was a tangled mess of teenagers holding red plastic cups and each other, swaying lazily, drunkenly, as rock blared from speakers positioned in separate corners. Smoke swirled above their heads and the smell of pepperoni, or maybe pizza, drifted from somewhere down the hallway.

"Come on," she said, ignoring Ellie's small gasp and pulling her toward the kitchen. "I bet Steve's down here."

"Who's Steve?" Ellie repeated the question as she stumbled after Chloe down the carpeted hallway, scrunching her nose at the sight of an abandoned red cup on the floor, its yellow liquid mixed with the butts of several cigarettes. "Eww," she said, but Chloe didn't hear.

"Hey Steve!" Chloe dropped Ellie's arm and walked toward a scruffily dressed male propped against the counter, his face partially concealed by a baseball cap pulled low and the hood on his sweatshirt pulled tight. Everything he wore was black, from the leather on his boots to the visor poking from his hoodie to his baggy jeans and belt. The only color he wore was a dark green emblem of a jagged-edged leaf positioned smack in the middle of the otherwise jet-black T-shirt beneath his unzipped hoodie. It was a neon green, and it shone strangely against all that black.

"Nice shirt," Chloe said, squeezing between a couple girls who were standing alongside him, sipping in between laughs from plastic cups. She gave him a hug and tapped the leaf image on his chest. "Got any?"

He gave a sly smile and pulled her head close for a kiss. His eyes fell on Ellie, and a look of wonder washed over his face. He ran his eyes first up her legs, her sides, her stomach, her neck, her face and hair, and then back down, all the way to her shoes, where he stared for several long moments.

With a sneer, he slowly raised his eyes to Ellie's face, then licked his lips.

"Who's your friend?"

Ellie shifted nervously in her taupe Mary Janes. She withered under his scrutiny, hugging herself tight while putting one foot in front of the other, then switching positions and putting the other foot in front of the first. The Mary Janes had been her favorites until that moment. Now, she wished for something less ladylike, some black leather boots, perhaps, or something with silver studs, like those on the girl in the corner blowing smoke from a white cigarette.

He was still staring. Stupidly, she stuck out her hand.

"Hi," she said, her tongue thick and slow in her mouth. "Hi. I'm—I'm—I'm Ellie," she finally said.

He opened his eyes wide and chuckled. Pulling a white and gold box from the pocket of his hoodie, he cracked the top and extended it to her. Embarrassed, she let her arm fall back to her side.

"Hello there, I'm, I'm, I'm Ellie," he said. "Cigarette?"

Ellie didn't trust her voice. She shook her head and shifted in her shoes once again.

"They don't smoke back down on the farm where you come from?" His imitation Southern accent cut through all the chatter in the kitchen and immediately, all eyes turned to Ellie. Steve looked at his audience with a pleased smile.

"Or maybe your daddy don't let his precious lil girl get that tabaccy on her smiley white teeth."

The room erupted with laughter and Ellie sunk deep into her Mary Janes, feeling her face blaze hot and hoping her cheeks weren't bright red. She stole a glance at Chloe for help. Chloe grinned, then smacked Steve on the shoulder.

"Leave her alone, Steve. She's new."

He gazed at Ellie for a moment in silence, then pushed away Chloe's hand.

"You headed to church?" he laughed, flicking ashes onto the floor. "I never seen a dress that covered up that much of a person's body—outside maybe those dressing gowns they wore 100 years ago. You get that from your grandmother?" He laughed, looking at the smiling faces who were egging him on. "That's it, isn't it. That was a birthday present from your grandmother. Or, maybe a hand-me-down. Maybe it was something your grandmother used to wear, then she died and left it to you." He took a deep drag on his cigarette, then threw the butt into the sink. Straightening, he pulled Chloe into his chest and hugged tight. He fixed Ellie with a cold, blank stare.

"You shoulda let the dress die with her."

"No!" Ellie shouted the first thing that came to her mind. Then for the second time in as many minutes, she felt stupid as they all stared. Chloe pushed back from Steve and stepped toward Ellie.

"Hey," she said, flicking her lightly on the shoulder, "I'm going to get some punch. You want some? It's good."

"Punch? You mean like juice?"

Chloe shot a sly smile at Steve.

"Yeah, like juice. It's a house special. It's red punch mixed with some other juice and limes. Look." She picked up a half-filled cup from the counter and held it so Ellie could see. "See all the lime slices? It's probably even healthy."

"Oh." Ellie sniffed. "Okay. It smells good anyway."

Chloe leaned back toward Steve and whispered in his ear.

"Sure. Here you go," he said, slipping something into her hand. Chloe gave him a long kiss, then playfully punched his shoulder.

"I'll give it back in a minute," she said, sliding her hand into her pocket. She turned to Ellie and nodded. "Give me just a minute. I have to use the bathroom, then we can get some punch."

Ellie nervously watched her leave.

A couple of the girls were seated on the kitchen countertops, their arms wrapped around their boyfriends, whose bodies were pressed tightly between their legs. Smoke filled the air and somebody dropped a cup to the floor. Ellie watched as yellow liquid oozed onto the tile, making tiny little rivers that slowed as they spread. When the flow stopped, she looked up to see if anyone was going to clean up the mess. She was surprised to see Steve standing so close.

"Hey there," he said, slurring as his body rocked slightly.

In a panic, Ellie looked over her shoulder for Chloe.

But Chloe was still making her way up the stairs to the bathroom, stepping over a girl who was sprawled on the fifth step and remarking rather dryly to another who was descending, "She shouldn't have worn such a short dress." The other girl laughed.

"Bathroom's on the right," she said, grabbing hold of Chloe for balance as she pointed toward the sky.

"Thanks." Chloe checked her pocket for the stuff Steve gave her; once reassured, she finished the climb to the upstairs. The bathroom door was locked. Chloe waited, knocked again, then waited some more, and knocked one more time.

"Other people gotta use it too, y'know!" She stepped into a nearby bedroom and shut the door.

"This is even better," she said to herself, as she pulled a small pipe and tightly rolled plastic sandwich bag out of her pocket. She unrolled the bag, shook the contents and watched as the tiny green flakes smacked against plastic. She smiled as she pinched a generous portion and felt nothing but flakes between her fingers. Steve always had the cleanest stuff. Opening the bedroom window, Chloe leaned her head out and flicked her lighter against the pipe. Drawing in deeply, she felt an explosion of joy and wondered what he laced it with this time.

Whatever it was, she thought lazily, sucking again at the pipe, it was great. She shut her eyes and blew, then opened them to a wonder of white billows wafting before her. Instead of fading and disappearing, as normal clouds do, these billows floated toward her, aiming at her, encircling her, wrapping her in a white gauzy glow, surrounding her, entering her.

She rubbed her arms, feeling a strange, electric warmth coursing through her veins. She let her hands slide to her ribcage and felt the points of her fingertips as they traced the warmth of the whiteness that had permeated her body. She lifted her left hand slowly and spread the fingers wide, watching as electric lines sprung forth from the tips—lines in the air sparkling with colors, that then became circles, then became bubbles that surrounded her, tickled her, lifted her off the ground. Was she flying? She couldn't be sure, but it felt as if she were and she didn't dare open her eyes in case she wasn't. She couldn't stand the disappointment. Not another life disappointment. She smiled at the sensation and lifted her arms like wings. She uncuffed fingers, let the pipe drop from her hand, and listened as it fell down, down, down, ricocheting off rocks of the great mountain she now shared with the eagles.

She peeled open her eyes, just a little, and sighed with joy at the blasts of colors and explosions of music that came with each ping of the pipe on rock. The colors then mixed with the musical notes, blends of blues and yellows and oranges all forming droplets that curiously, fell upward. Chloe reached with cautious hands and tried to grab them as they passed. But they melted and dropped like gobs of water onto the mountainside, only to splash over the rocks, falling, falling to an unseen fate.

Chloe had no idea how long she watched the tumult of color.

But when she finally came down from the mountain, the first things she saw was Ellie's face, twisted and wet with tears. The flowers on Ellie's dress were ripped and black mascara streaked her cheeks. Chloe stared, confused, trying to make sense of the frayed cloth at Ellie's shoulder and the physical jerking she felt within her own body. It took some seconds for Chloe to realize Ellie was shaking her frantically and screaming at her.

She blinked hard and fought to make out Ellie's words.

"Wake up! Wake up! I want to go home! Take me home now, Chloe!"

CHLOE

Ellie wasn't in school Monday, or the next day, or the next after that. Sometime later, maybe a month or two after the party, Chloe overheard a couple girls in the bathroom talking about that stupid Jesus freak suddenly moving away. They didn't say the girl's name. But Chloe, with a sinking feeling in her stomach, knew it was Ellie. She never found out what happened at the party.

CHAPTER FOUR

"GOD LOVES YOU."

Chloe looked down at the paper receipt in her hand and blinked once, twice, then a third time. She read the black block letters in disbelief. It was tough enough paying rent, even when tips were good. "GOD LOVES YOU."

"What the—" she started, then looked quickly around, making sure her other customers didn't hear.

She looked out the window just in time to see her customer, a man dressed all in black, including a black hat with an oversized floppy brim, slide into the driver's seat of his car. He paused, staring her way. Then he gave a strange little smile and waved as he drove off, his hat angled so it shadowed much of his face.

Angrily, Chloe shoved the receipt into her apron pocket and swept into her hand bits of French fries and hamburger bun crumbs from the table he just left. She gave it a quick wipe with her dampened towel, tossed the ketchup and mustard bottles into the dark gray bin she balanced against her hip, then set two plastic menus in their metal holders alongside the salt and pepper shakers. She looked through the diner window at his car as he pulled from the lot.

The guy gave her the creeps. There was something very familiar about him, especially in his eyes. They were icy blue-gray in color, but they seemed to change to gold when

63

he spoke, and at one point, when Chloe was serving his coffee and placing the mug on the table, she glanced at his eyes and thought she saw dancing figures in his tiny irises. Shocked, she stopped pouring and gazed. Then, the image disappeared and all that was left was the face of an elderly man with long, unruly hair and a disheveled beard and a floppy faded black hat. Angrily, she pushed his coffee mug toward him. She searched her mind for hints of where she knew him but came up empty. The mystery made her fume and she thrust open the swinging door to the back room with such intensity it smashed against the wall and left a dent in the paint.

"Another stiff," she said, as she tossed her rag toward the corner of the kitchen, missing the bucket. She plopped on a milk crate and watched as Marjorie sifted through the freezer and pulled out two frozen chicken patties.

She held them to the light for inspection.

"I can't believe we feed our customers this crap," Marjorie said, shutting the freezer door with a clunk. "Fresh food, my ass."

Chloe snorted and shrugged.

"Guess I'm not going with you guys tonight," Chloe said sullenly. "I got stiffed again."

"Are you serious?" Marjorie popped her bleach-blonde head from the freezer and snapped her gum loudly at Chloe. "That guy dressed in black didn't leave you anything?"

For answer, Chloe kicked at a box of canned green beans on the floor. Marjorie stepped back from the freezer and looked down at Chloe with sympathy. She stood in silence for a few moments, unsure what to say. Then she grabbed her bag from her locker and yanked over the zipper.

"Wanna have a smoke?"

Chloe shrugged and pulled her apron off her waist. Tossing it carelessly on the floor by the green beans, she shrugged again.

"I freaking quit," she said.

"Come on," Marjorie said, rifling for her lighter as she held tightly to a box of Marlboros. "You know you can't quit. Let's just go smoke." She glanced through the glass on the door to the near-empty dining area. "Come on," she said again. "Tony won't miss us."

Chloe glanced through the window of the kitchen door at the cook, Tony, busily scraping at his grill with a spatula. An elderly man wearing a red-checked wool jacket sat nursing a cup of coffee at the counter. The only other customers were a heavy-set woman with frizzy hair and her equally frizzy-haired little girl. They had just been served their waffles and fried chicken.

Chloe regarded them coolly.

More customers to screw me on the tip, no doubt, she thought.

"Fine." She stood and followed Marjorie to the back door. The cold slapped their faces hard and Chloe sucked in her breath sharply.

"Man, I hate this weather," she said, hopping from one foot to another and rubbing her arms.

"Well, you could've grabbed your coat, dummy," Marjorie held out her cigarette pack to Chloe, then just as quickly, pulled it away. "You know, this is like the third cigarette I've given you today. How about buying your own pack?"

"I'm quitting. You know that." Chloe's teeth chattered as she watched Marjorie flick her lighter. "Especially now since I'm unemployed. I won't be able to afford 'em anymore."

Marjory grunted and re-extended the box to Chloe.

"Oh come on, you know you're not quitting your job. How would you buy your booze if you didn't have any money?" Marjorie laughed mischievously. "I mean, you seriously can't quit and give up all that money you make from tips. Your customers love you so much."

Chloe breathed in deeply and stared at Marjorie in silence for a few seconds. It was a well-known joke among the wait staff at the diner that Chloe wasn't the friendliest of servers and customers often expressed their dissatisfaction with measly tips.

Chloe shrugged and, pursing her lips into the shape of a tight little circle, she blew smoke hard directly into Marjorie's face, smiling as her friend coughed and choked.

"Maybe I'll just hook up with Jay. He's been wanting me to move in with him for a while now. I'll live with him and drink all his beer," Chloe finally said. She took another drag and added, more to herself than to Marjorie, "But I gave that guy great service today. I don't know why he stiffed me."

"Jay? That looooser?" Marjorie said, ignoring the second comment Chloe made. "That's pretty desperate."

"Hey. Desperate times call for desperate measures. And times are definitely getting desperate." Chloe slipped her hand into her pants pocket. "You wanna see what that jerk left me instead of a tip?"

She pulled out a crumpled paper and smoothed it so Marjorie could better see.

"Look at that."

Marjorie squinted and then wrinkled her nose.

"God loves you? What is that?" She laughed so hard her voice went dry and she started to cough.

"I know, right? No tip. But God loves you." Chloe grunted and shoved the paper back in her pocket. "Apparently, God doesn't love me or He would've given me a $100 tip."

"At least a few dollars' tip. I mean, didn't he order like $50 worth of food?"

"It was $64.93 exactly. He ordered like three different meals and all these sides. He had fish and chips, he had the big breakfast with toast, he had the Caesar salad with extra dressing, then he had a separate plate of pancakes and a side of raisin toast—he had all this crap, plus a milkshake, plus iced tea, plus coffee. It was like breakfast, lunch, and dinner, all at once. Then," Chloe said dramatically, lifting her hand as she spoke, "then—then he didn't even eat half of it. He left it on the table."

She finished her cigarette and dropped the butt on the ground.

"For me to clean," she said bitterly, grinding her boot on the filter, until it was flat against the ice.

"That sucks," Marjorie said, stomping out her cigarette and pulling open the door. Almost brightly, she asked, "So, you can't go tonight?"

Chloe watched as Marjorie pulled a small mirror out of her purse and fluffed the front of her hair then turned her face to check her makeup. She frowned slightly then grabbed a stick of mascara and expertly flitted black onto her lashes. She fished through her purse and muttered, "That's too bad, maybe another time," then with a wide smile, pulled out a bright red lipstick. "That's too bad," she said again, smacking her lips and rubbing them together as she angled the mirror in the light. Satisfied, she held the lipstick out to Chloe. Chloe shook her head and Marjorie dropped the lipstick back in her bag and slammed it shut with a loud click.

"So," she said, picking at something in her teeth, "I guess I can give your ticket to someone else then?"

Chloe regarded her gloomily. The concert was the only thing keeping her going all week—all month, really. Marjorie won the tickets in a radio contest and asked Chloe to be the blind date for her boyfriend's friend, with the condition to split the travel costs of taxi service to the event.

Expecting to use her most recent waitressing tips for the taxi, Chloe spent the last of her savings on a killer dress and matching shoes. It had been a long time since she went on anything like a date. Most of her weekends were spent at the bar, sucking down as many drinks as she could get somebody else to buy for her. It wasn't hard. She learned long ago how a short dress and flirty smile bought as much alcohol as her liver could take. Usually, she wouldn't even remember the things she did later at the guy's house to repay him for his generosity. The concert was going to be her glimpse of the good life—a nice dinner, a fun night, a real date.

She scowled and cursed the man in the floppy black hat.

"Yeah, go ahead. I'm about broke," Chloe said softly, bitterness filling her heart at the thought of her stingy customers.

"That sucks," Marjorie said again, holding the door open for Chloe. "But no biggie. I'll just get one of my other friends to go instead."

Chloe grimaced at Marjorie's cheery tone, and for a second, considered asking for a loan. The taxi was $50 or so each way; Chloe hadn't counted the money in her pocket from her morning customers, but she knew it wasn't anywhere near the amount she needed for her portion of the expenses. But then Marjorie, as if reading her thoughts, said, "I wish I had the money to loan you, but I don't," and Chloe's face fell. She stopped at the doorway, then reached for her coat, hanging on a hook just inches away.

Marjorie turned curiously and watched as Chloe pulled up the zipper.

"Hey, wouldya tell Tony I don't feel too good. Tell him I went home to catch up on my sleep." It was half true. The thought of her new dress, hanging in its clear plastic bag in her closet, was giving her an upset stomach. It was too fancy to wear to her normal weekend bar spots, but too expensive to just toss to Goodwill. Chloe knew it would probably sit there, untouched, unworn, mocking, for months to come.

Again, she spit out a curse at the man in black.

"Stupid customers," she mumbled, letting the door swing behind her. Marjorie shot out a hand to keep it from closing.

"I'll see you Monday. Hey, will I see you Monday?" Her voice floated through the crack, but Chloe didn't bother to answer.

She climbed into her car, spinning her tires in the packed snow as she peeled from the parking lot onto the highway toward home. She drove recklessly, her disappointment and anger blotting out any hesitations she may have had about passing vehicles that dared get in her way. Her tires slipped on the slushy frozen road, but she brazenly pushed even harder on the accelerator pedal. On impulse, she pulled into the convenience store at the roadside corner, about a mile from her home.

She jumped from her car and stormed inside, ignoring the shocked expression of the young man working the counter.

"Pack of Marlboros," she said, plopping some bills on the counter before reaching into her pocket to count change. Peering over her shoulder, then back at the handful of quarters in her hand, she mumbled as she walked away, "Wait a minute," then strode to the cooler section and peered at the stacks of cans. She let her finger slide along the glass, scrolling down the selection of beers until she found one in her price range.

"Yessss," she whispered triumphantly, grabbing it and returning to the counter, where she slammed it so hard the cashier jumped. She kept her eyes on her hand, counting and recounting the bits of change splayed across her palm, as she waited anxiously for him to announce the total. She sighed with relief as he said, "That'll be $6.92."

"Here you go," she said brusquely, thrusting out a closed fist and dropping four bills and twelve quarters into his palm. Quickly, she turned to leave, but then thought better of it and decided to wait for the few pennies in change instead.

Chloe stared out the window as the cashier clinked each coin into the register, counting out slowly and stopping now and again to poke the change in his hand. She bit her tongue in impatience and fought the urge to ask him if he was an idiot. Finally, he finished and held out a cupped hand toward Chloe.

"Eight cents is your change," he said, dropping the coins into her palm. Chloe turned and left without saying a word. She climbed into her car and was about to shove the change into her pocket, when something made her look. Sighing with frustration, she saw the clerk gave her a quarter instead of a nickel.

"Moron!" She got out of the car and slammed the door tight.

"This is a quarter," she said, slapping it down and pushing it toward the cashier. "You meant to give me a dime."

He stared for several seconds in silence. Chloe tapped her fingers impatiently on the countertop and wondered why she hadn't just driven off with the money. It wasn't like her to care about something as piddly as a quarter, and while she hadn't stolen from stores in years, she wasn't exactly morally opposed to the idea. Stealing was just something she sort of grew out of, like old clothes, and really, the reason she outgrew it was probably her free time was more often spent in bars than in shopping malls. It was tough to steal while drunk.

Chloe cleared her throat and tried to peer at his face, half hidden by long hair dangling over his cheeks.

"Uh, hello?" She gestured toward the quarter. "My dime?"

He looked up with a smile so wide and eyes glinting so brightly that Chloe took a step back from the counter. His gray-blue eyes swept over her and Chloe gasped in surprise. They were the color of the man's eyes who stiffed her that morning. Confused, she frowned.

"Here you go!" She watched as he scooped up the quarter, tapped open the register, and pulled something out. Gingerly, palm cupped, he extended a long, narrow index finger toward Chloe and when she looked, she saw balanced on the tip was a single shiny dime. It glistened in the light and Chloe watched the rays dance before she reached out a tentative hand. The air suddenly smelled of vanilla, and Chloe looked around for the source.

"Not many people would bother," he said, his eyes, now glittery green, locking with Chloe's as he dropped the dime into her hand. "You're very honest."

Chloe snorted. *Honest* was not a word she was used to people calling her.

"Really?" Her fingers closed around the dime and she pursed her lips in scorn. She was about to say something else when she caught another whiff of vanilla and she turned her head in surprise, expecting to see some fresh baked cookies or cakes on the counter. Save for a display of headache medicines and cell phone charges, though, the counter was clear.

He straightened and rubbed his beard, a thick golden patch covering his entire chin, and regarded her silently, his eyes dancing with laughter.

What's up with the beards today? she wondered idly, as her mind flashed to the man in the diner. The memory made her scowl and she turned to leave. All she wanted was to drink her beer and forget about the day.

"Hey, God bless you," he called with a smile, as she pushed through the door. She hesitated, just a second, and then without turning, let go the door and kept walking. Right before the glass settled on its frame, her ears caught his parting call.

"God loves you!"

She bit her tongue to keep from shouting back a couple of choice curse words. *What is it with the 'God loves you'?* she thought furiously. She couldn't wait to get home.

Chloe slipped behind the wheel and tore the wrapper off her cigarettes, flicking her lighter several times until it finally sparked. She sucked in deeply as she turned the ignition and her car sprang to life.

"Freaking Jesus freaks," she mumbled, forgetting in the light of the store's signage to put on her headlights. "What'd God ever do for me?"

She stopped at the edge of the parking lot and reached for the beer she tossed on the passenger seat. With a quick glance for police cruisers, she popped open the can and swallowed hungrily, the faces of bearded men flashing in her mind.

"Freaking Jesus freaks and their 'God loves you,'" she said mockingly, taking another drink and another drag of her cigarette.

"Let's get some music on in here," she said out loud, snapping the volume on high and bobbing her head to the blaring rock song.

She sang a few notes, then took one more sip and pulled into the road, accelerating until the engine whined. She saw it from the corner of her eye, a flash of dark red and black, and instinctively, swerved to the right.

"Son of a—!" she didn't finish.

Her right front tire struck a pothole and the sudden jolt caused her beer can to fly from her hand. Beer swished onto her lap and she pulled again on the wheel. A sharp pain filled her mouth as she bit hard on her tongue, and with a cry, she felt her fingers open and saw her cigarette drop.

The crash jerked her head back and to the side, off the steering wheel into the headrest, and she felt it twist uncomfortably as it came to rest on her shoulder. Her legs crumpled somewhere beneath the gnarled metal and plastic of the dash, while her right arm jammed deep into her ribs, cutting off her breathing. Her wrist felt as if it had been thrust in the middle of a roaring blaze and for one confused moment, with the rock music still blaring in the background, she roamed her eyes desperately for a bottle of water to put out the flames. She took in the shards of glass, the bent steering wheel, the broken knobs, and vents in dull shock.

Then it dawned on her what had happened.

She lifted her bruised head and with great effort, peeked through the space her windshield used to occupy and her gaze fell on a dark reddish-colored van with a rumpled front end, spewing smoke from its hood.

"I'm in a crash," she said out loud.

Her last thought, as her head drooped and she drifted into unconsciousness, was of the words from a yellow bumper sticker on the van that were illuminated by its one working taillight: "God Loves You."

"What's your name, sweetie?"

The voice came out of the darkness and slowly, Chloe peeled open her eyes. Bright light flooded and she squinted painfully. Her entire body was sore and she started to take stock, from the numbness of her left foot, up the throbbing in her leg, over to the grinding throb in her hip and up the small of her back, and finally, to the thudding in her head. She couldn't tell if it was coming from behind her eye, or from her forehead, but it pounded and she flexed her hand to reach up and touch it, then cried out loud. Her wrist was on fire. It felt like someone was stabbing at it with a red-hot knife, sticking in the blade then holding it to her skin until the heat seared her flesh, then pulling it out and jabbing again. With difficulty, she glanced to her hand and saw in its place, a ball of white gauzy cloth layers so thick it looked like a small balloon.

"You okay, dear?" Chloe felt a pat on her shoulder and turned toward the source, moaning again as her neck muscles screamed.

A woman in green hospital scrubs and dark hair pulled tightly from her face held a clipboard. She scribbled for several moments then looked at Chloe, stretched on the bed, a bewildered expression on her face.

"You've been in a car accident," she said, patting Chloe on the shoulder again.

Chloe just looked at her, waiting.

"Can you tell me your name, sweetie?" Chloe nodded, once, twice, but still said nothing, the burn in her wrist so intense she couldn't pry open her pursed lips.

"Well," the woman in scrubs said. "What is it?"

"Chloe," she finally said.

"Good. And your last name?"

Chloe thought hard then swallowed, feeling the thickness of her tongue against the back of her throat.

"Richards," she said weakly. She closed her eyes in exhaustion.

"And the year?" The woman waited, her pencil poised above the clipboard. Chloe kept her eyes shut, hoping the woman would give up and leave.

"And the year, Chloe?" The nurse scratched something on her clipboard with her pen, but then waited as Chloe opened then shut her eyes several times.

Chloe tilted her head toward her and whispered again.

"Good. Yes, that's right." She scribbled more. "You seem like you're coming out of it well."

Coming out of what, Chloe thought dully, but she hadn't the strength to ask, and as she watched the nurse walk about, adjusting first this tube and then that, she thought perhaps she didn't really want to know.

It didn't matter; the nurse took up a spot to the right of Chloe and started chatting in rapid-fire fashion.

CHLOE

"Your leg is broken so try not to move it," she said. "You also have a nasty break on your left wrist, and the doctor wants to talk to you about some complications that might come during healing. You could end up having more surgery to restore your range of motion fully. But the doctor will be around later today and you can ask him more about that."

She paused to consult a stack of papers on her clipboard.

"You'll probably be sore and swollen all over for a little while, probably on your neck and back too, and it'll take some time for all your cuts to heal. Hopefully, you won't have a serious concussion, but your head where you hit it on the steering wheel will be sore for a time, and you might get headaches for a while." She rifled and slapped the papers so loudly Chloe's eyes widened in surprise.

"I'll be back to change your bandages or another nurse will do it soon. The doctor was in once about an hour ago, but you'll probably have a chance to speak to him before his shift ends. He should be back soon."

Chloe, perplexed, said nothing.

The nurse reached under the bed covers to move something, and Chloe groaned at the sudden pressure in her groin area.

"That's the catheter," the nurse said, patting down the blanket and sifting tubing through her fingers. "And you'll probably have to go for a CT scan later today. It just depends on when the doctor comes by to check on you."

Chloe nodded as best she could, unsure what questions she should be asking, or if she already asked the questions that needed to be asked, but just couldn't remember their answers. An image of her car flashed suddenly in her mind, and she started to ask where it was, but the pain in her chest cut off her words. She shut her eyes and breathed as lightly as possible, deciding she didn't need to know about her car right then, after all.

"You know, the police are going to want to talk to you."

Chloe's head involuntarily turned toward the nurse and she gulped back a scream, wishing she hadn't moved her neck so quickly.

"Police?" Chloe reached with her good hand to rub her neck. "What do you mean?"

Her eyes followed the woman's pointed finger to the other side of the room, to the crack in the curtain and the uniformed officer standing at the desk and sipping from a white Styrofoam cup. Chloe watched as he bent a brown-haired head and carefully removed the lid, releasing a torrent of steam. Then he took a step or two to the left and his body disappeared from view, and all Chloe could see was a pair of shiny black shoes below a cuff of dark pants peeking from the space beneath the curtain. She stifled another groan, this one, only partially from pain.

That's just great, she thought, settling her head on her pillow and trying to recall the day's events.

"Your blood test hasn't come back yet," the nurse said, her pen making scratching noises on the clipboard as she noted numbers on the machine Chloe was hooked to and made adjustments. Her voice was pleasant, but rather businesslike and Chloe wondered if that was her natural tone or if the police officer at the desk said something about the circumstances of her car wreck. Chloe scrunched her nose, trying to remember what happened.

"But when they do," the nurse said, "we'll have to report the results to the authorities."

Chloe gave her a quizzical look and the nurse stared back sternly.

"They said they found an empty beer can in your car," she said coldly. Chloe groaned inwardly. *The officer talked. Now all the nurses hate me.*

"Anyway," the nurse said, her tone again chipper, "it's just standard we check your blood alcohol level in cases like this."

Chloe turned her eyes to the black television set mounted on the wall in front of her. She was done with the nurse. Whatever happened, would happen. She stared at the TV, waited for the woman to finish, and pretended to not hear when she asked about her family members and her health insurance, and which friend or relative might be able to pick her up when she was discharged. After a minute, the nurse got the message and worked in silence.

"Okay, I guess that's it," she said, flipping the metal cover closed on the clipboard and hanging it expertly from a hook at the foot of Chloe's bed.

She turned, then hesitated at the door.

"Is it okay if I send the officer in now to talk to you?"

Chloe didn't look away from the television set. But after a moment, she gave a slight nod, and shut her eyes.

"Right, better to get it over with. That's right." Her voice was softer and she stepped toward Chloe to give her a quick, comforting pat. Then Chloe heard the whisk of the curtain and opened her eyes to an empty room.

But she could see the white, thick-soled shoes of the nurse beneath the curtain and she watched as they stood near the desk, alongside the black ones worn by the police officer. Their voices drifted into the room, too low for Chloe to make out what they were saying. Then she saw the white shoes turn and heard the soft clop of rubber on floor as they disappeared from view. A few seconds later, the black shoes turned, pointed toes to Chloe's room, and she followed them as they moved to the curtain. She shut her eyes as the curtain swished and kept them shut, even as she heard the rather loud slide of metal hooks on a metal rod, then the click, click of the officer's shoes as he approached her bed.

"Chloe Richards?"

His voice was clear, and loud. She couldn't pretend not to hear. She turned weakly toward him, taking in his crisp blue uniform and short, clipped hair. He held a notebook in one hand, and a pen and cap in the other. His eyes were brown, calm, and businesslike. Her first impression was he was somebody who shouldn't be crossed.

She shifted to try a sitting position, then immediately regretted it. He stood silent as she moaned out loud then rubbed her wrapped wrist with the index finger of her other hand, trying to soothe the burn. After a few futile moments, she stopped rubbing and turned her head toward him. His expression hadn't changed.

"Chloe Richards?" He waited for her to nod. "Is that your name?" She nodded again and he beckoned to the chair in the corner of the room. "Mind if I sit for a few minutes? I need to ask you a few questions about your accident. That okay?"

He sat before she could answer.

"Sure," she said anyway, watching through tired eyes as he opened his notebook and started jotting something in pen.

He fixed her with a blank stare.

"Were you drinking alcohol at the time of your accident?"

Terror gripped her heart and her eyes widened in fear. She remembered what the nurse said about the empty beer can in her car, and wondered if the officer knew about it. *Of course he knew about it*, she thought, in a panic. *Don't be stupid. How could he not know about it? He was the one who told the nurse.*

She felt dizzy and hot and fought to choke back her emotions, afraid that if she weren't careful, if she didn't stay calm, it wouldn't matter what words she said because the police officer would see the fright in her face and know the truth and she'd be arrested for a DUI on the spot.

In jail by five, she thought sardonically, stealing a glance at the clock on the wall.

She felt trapped, like a frightened rabbit surrounded by a frenzy of dogs. She felt the pain growing in her back, in her hip, in her leg. She felt tears welling in the corner of her eyes, and frustration that her hand hurt too much to wipe them away.

"Chloe?"

She said the only thing she could think to say that made sense to her in the moment.

"I don't remember," she said. "I don't know."

She breathed out slowly and repeated it, growing more convinced of it herself.

"I just don't remember. I don't know."

CHAPTER FIVE

Chloe pushed away the food tray in disgust, slapping the thin bread slice back on the plain pink bologna slab and upsetting her fruit cup in the process. Watery juice spilled on her plate, seeping into her perfectly formed circle of mashed potatoes. She picked up a plastic fork and poked the now-pinkish potatoes, then tossed the utensil back on the plate and crossed her arms angrily. Her wrist burned, making her even angrier.

Was this hospital food or prison food? She wasn't hungry anyway. She stared hard out the window, as if something were there, just beyond her line of vision, something that could save her. Raindrops slithered down the glass and for a moment, she was a little girl again, watching droplets of water or melted snow race down the windowpanes of her room and guessing which would come in first, which would come in second, all while the sound of her parents' drunken arguments played in the background.

She shook her head and looked with a grimace again at her food. As bad as things now seemed, she still didn't wish for a return to childhood.

Stupid cop, she thought, tears springing to her eyes. *Stupid cops.*

Chloe rubbed her head against her pillow and let out a deep sigh. *What to do now?* She ruffled the paperwork in her hand, a small pile of pink and white and yellow sheets presented to her by the police officer who had just left. He was fatter and shorter than the first officer who questioned her days ago in her same hospital room. His shoes weren't as shiny either.

Earlier, Chloe watched as they clicked back and forth beneath the curtain hem, the leather more gray than black, one shoelace dangling so far it touched the floor. The pacing made her nervous, as did the sound of the pacing—a steady click, clack, click, clack. But she kept watching them just the same.

She kept watching because there was nothing else to watch.

After two weeks in the same hospital room, she had counted every block on the wall, every seam in the ceiling, every section of the window blinds, every wire, tube, knob, and container within her line of sight, and with the exception of the shows on the television, nothing changed. Everything was the same. And even when she did turn on the TV, the shows were all alike. News in the morning, sports in the afternoon, news at night, mindless reality shows in between. She longed for some excitement, and barring that, for something—anything—that wasn't the same.

Bitterly, she looked at the gray leather shoes still standing by the desk, belonging to the body of the police officer beyond the curtain she could no longer see.

He had given her something different to do, she thought crossly, biting back tears again.

She looked at the packet of papers in her hand with utter hopelessness.

Each page was a condemnation of how badly she'd screwed up her life. Each page also brought a messy, expensive punishment she knew she'd never be able to pay. She ticked off the totals in her mind: $350 for driving with an open container of alcohol; $120 for reckless driving; $200 for reckless driving resulting in an accident; $60 for failure to yield; $50 for improper signaling. Then came the court summons for her alcohol-related charges, and the accompanying court costs. She glanced at the information sheet the police officer stuck to the bottom of the packet. Just for the pleasure of stepping in court would cost her $35; after that, she'd have to pay $100 for the hearing before the judge; after that, more costs could come depending on which way the judge ruled. *All that*, she thought ruefully, *without even figuring the cost of an attorney*.

She looked at the other papers in her hand—a police brochure that talked about the costs of driving under the influence and included such warnings as insurance cancellations and license revocations. She groaned at the thought of losing her license.

Then she remembered the officer's words.

"Your car was towed and impounded, but it looks like it was totaled anyway. It's $100 a day to store, so you might want to call your insurance company," he said.

What difference does it make if I have a driver's license if I have no car to drive, she thought.

Her curtain swept open and startled, Chloe looked up then quickly wiped her eyes.

"I just wanted to let you know before I leave that if the doctor doesn't give you the okay to leave the hospital before your court date, be sure and call the clerk's office and request a new hearing time. If you miss your date, the judge will order an arrest warrant and I'll have to come pick you up—then you'll have to pay the costs of service too," the police officer said.

Chloe nodded and watched his gray shoes until they disappeared from view.

She let the papers sink onto her lap, not caring when a couple of the pages slipped off and floated to the floor.

Her eyes filled with water and tears streamed down her face. She had zero money, zero transportation, and probably zero waitressing job. Soon to come, she knew, was zero home.

A black, heavy cloud settled in her mind, and through a watery haze, all she saw was darkness. Her shoulders sagged on the pillow and she began to sob.

I'm so stupid, she thought, over and over and over, a mantra she emphasized with memories of her stupidity—of the time she got caught stealing, of the time her mother locked her in the closet for two days as punishment, of the time her father slapped her so hard he broke her front tooth, of the time her classmates threw brown paper bags at her and told her to put them over her face. She sniffled hard, and rubbed her nose to stop it from running. Her cheeks burned with hot tears.

I'm so freaking stupid. I'm so freaking stupid.

She searched desperately on her table, on the nurse's table, beneath her tray for any pills, any medicines, anything at all, even poisonous, she could ingest and stop the anguish. But she knew nothing was there. She knew her search was in vain. And the fact she knew that but searched anyway gave her even more reason to keep up the mantra.

I'm so stupid, she thought. *I'm so stupid.*

She didn't know how long she went on that way, but when her tears finally stopped, her eyes felt raw and swollen, her jaw was sore from clenching so tight and her wrist, the wrapped wrist that still hurt so much that the pain kept her up at night—her wrist was pounding with such intensity she couldn't tell where one throb started and another throb ended. Her throat was dry and begged for water, but she was too tired and despondent to lift her head and turn even six inches to suck on the straw in the filled plastic cup on her bedside table.

Never in her life, not even in her childhood, when all was dark, and the darkness was all the time, never had Chloe felt such gloom. Never had she felt this worthless.

Her leg burned, her hip burned, her wrist burned, almost as much as her heart, and she gripped tight with her one good hand the side rail of her bed, wishing she could just somehow end it.

She clamped her eyes tight and drew her breath deep and did something she could never before in her life remember doing.

She prayed.

God, she thought, sniffing at the runny stuff trickling from her nostrils—*God, if You're real, help me. Help me, help me, please, help me.* She repeated it over and over in her mind, finally whispering it out loud, growing more and more forceful with each whisper until she was speaking at a normal tone of voice. She leaned forward in her bed as much as her pain would allow, bent her head, and squeezed her eyelids tight.

"God, help me. Please. If You're real, if You're really there, help me. Please."

Her head shot up at the sound of a click, and suddenly, light flickered from the television set. Her mouth fell open in surprise. A man's booming voice filled the room.

"God loves you!"

Chloe stared at the screen, at the gray-haired man in the blue suit as he walked the length of a blue-carpeted stage, stopping to look into the camera lens. His eyes seemed fixed on her own.

"So I say to you now," the man said, "to all those in darkness, all those in fear, to all those living in the uncertainty of the world and not in the bosom of God's grace—are you in need of mercy? Are you in need of forgiveness? Are you in need of protection and salvation from the enemy?"

Chloe listened, not understanding, but transfixed nevertheless.

He cupped his hand and extended a long, bony finger.

"Do you know that God loves you?" He paused and nodded vigorously. "Do you know how much God loves you!"

His finger was aimed right at Chloe and she held her breath, waiting.

"Do you know He's here, right now?" He swept his arm again. "Do you know He's listening to you, to your words, your thoughts—your heart." He thumped his open hand onto his chest. "He knows what you're feeling inside. He knows your troubles, your distresses. He knows, child, that you're in trouble."

Chloe choked back a gasp, then looked around to see if anyone heard her. The space beneath the curtain of her room was empty; she glanced at the clock and saw it was time for the nurses' shift change. They would be in a staff meeting, where the day nurses filled in the night nurses on what they needed to know about their patients. Nobody would be by for a half hour or so, Chloe knew. She turned back to the man on the TV.

He took a step toward her.

"Child," he said wrapping fingers from both hands around the microphone and dropping his head slightly, as if thinking deeply. Dramatically, he lifted his face and focused on the camera lens.

"When are you going to surrender? When are you going to let your past go, let your addictions go, let your alcohol go, let your drugs go, let your failures go, let your lousy life go—when are you going to let go of everything and realize you don't have to go it alone—you've never been alone a day in your life? There's a God who is the God of the universe—who made the entire universe—but He's also a God who cares so much for you, yes you, that He's counted every hair on your head? And He has a plan for your life filled with purpose and joy, if you just let Him lead?"

Chloe, swept by the cadence, nodded lightly.

"God has been there from the beginning. He's there with you now." The man smiled and lifted a hand in the air, arm stretched high. "And He'll be with you at the end. He will never leave you nor forsake you. So surrender. Let go the darkness and accept Him as your Savior—accept Jesus Christ into your heart and let Him bear the weight of your burdens."

How? Chloe puzzled over his words, scrunching her nose as she tried to make sense of what it meant to surrender, especially to something she couldn't even see—especially to something she wasn't even sure existed.

She pulled back a bit as the memory of her father's mocking jeers filled her mind. It was Christmas; she was a little girl. She couldn't remember how little, but little enough she actually believed Santa might bring her a present and that the present might be a puppy. The doorbell rang and Chloe, filled with visions of Santa holding her new puppy, raced to answer. Her face fell as she saw a man and woman at the door instead, holding not a dog but rather a big piece of paper. They smiled and were about to hand it to Chloe, when her father's booming voice gave them pause. He rounded the corner of the hallway and stomped to the door, beer can in hand, breath stinking of stale cigarettes, and snarled at the couple, "What the hell do you want." With surprise, Chloe watched as the woman's smile, rather than fade, only widened, and then with a happy little nod she reached and placed the paper into her father's hand.

"We hope you both can make it," she said, with a welcoming wink to Chloe.

"Merry Christmas," the man said, as they both turned to leave.

Her father glanced at the paper and burst into jeers of laughter.

"Church service! You think I wanna waste my time going to church on a day off of work?" He laughed at his own sarcasm, finished the beer, and crushed the can with one hand.

"There is no God!"

Her father balled up the paper and threw it at the woman's back. It bounced off her shoulder into the snow piled alongside the pathway to the front porch. Chloe saw her expression when she turned, and it was one she still remembered, a face of such sadness and pity, so out of place for a bright snowy Christmas day.

That had been the bulk of Chloe's experience with God.

But there was something about the man on the television set that touched Chloe and drove her to listen. She forgot her father and turned her ears to the preacher once again.

"Christ died on the cross so you might live—that's how much He loves you. So let go your fears, let go your flesh, let go your fleshly desires and give Him your troubles, give

Him your heart, turn your life to Him, and take the step of faith. Turn to Him now. Turn to the one who waits for you and take Him into your heart, accept Him into your life."

Chloe watched as the man spun and shook his finger back and forth in the air. She didn't understand what he meant by Christ dying on the cross; she heard people talk about it before, of course. But she did not understand the significance. As if listening to her thoughts, the man on the screen shouted out "Jesus!"—and turned once again to face the camera lens, looking directly into Chloe's face

"Do you know the meaning of the cross, child?" Shocked, Chloe shook her head.

"Jesus was without sin—He came to earth, was born as God's Son to a human mother, Mary. He took on the form of flesh, became a man, so He might feel what we all feel, suffer the same temptations of the body we all suffer—but He never sinned. He was perfect. And yet He willingly went to the cross for us all. He was crucified in complete innocence, absent any sin at all—even His thoughts were pure—and He did that to pay for our sins. He died on the cross to atone for humanity's sins, past, present, and future sins—all our sins."

Chloe's ears tingled and she felt a warmth in her body that was both strange and wonderful. It was like she was being hugged by someone with a very soft, light touch. But it was more than that. It was like she was being blanketed by something so light and airy, it could not be grasped, only experienced. She struggled to put words to her feelings. All that came to mind was an image from long ago, the eyes of a stranger she met on the street as she walked home from school; a man she had mostly forgotten over the years, but whose facial features she now recalled in vivid detail.

"Mr. Xander!" she said out loud, his dancing angelic eyes flashing before her. Surprised at her outburst, she looked around the room, half expecting to see him there.

"Don't let Satan win," the man on the television screen said. "Don't let the deceiver deceive you. As true as I'm standing here now, I say this to you with full faith and belief: There's a reason you're listening to me now. There's a reason you turned your television set on now. There's a reason you flipped through the channels and stopped to listen to this preaching right now. There's a reason you haven't moved on and shut me off—there's a reason you're listening, you're wondering, you're feeling the truth coming across these airwaves, into your ears, into your mind, into your heart."

Chloe, eyes glued on the set, nodded. She believed that too.

She waited, not moving, not realizing she was holding her breath, for him to tell her the reason.

"It's because God is speaking to you and He's telling you, child, the time is now," he said. "The Bible tells us He says, 'Behold, I stand at the door and knock; if anyone hears my voice and opens the door, I will come in to him and eat with him, and he with me.' Well, Jesus is at the door. Jesus is knocking at the door. The question is: Are you going to let Him in to be with you?"

Chloe swallowed hard. *Yes*, she thought. *But how?*

"The Bible tells us, in Romans, 'If you confess with your mouth the Lord Jesus and believe in your heart that God has raised Him from the dead you will be saved.' Do you know what that means? Do you know how to do that?" His eyes widened and he brought the microphone close to his lips, his hand trembling slightly as he spoke, louder now: "I invite you to do just that. I invite you to join God's Kingdom and leave the blackness of Satan's world behind. If you're hearing this message and you're not saved, join me now in this prayer—confess your sins and take Jesus into your life."

Chloe nodded again, ready.

"Say it with me," the man said. "Say this prayer: 'God, I know I have sinned, I know I'm a sinner, but I also know You have sent Your Son, Jesus, to die on the cross to pay for my sins. I accept that Jesus is my Savior, the One who died for my sins, the One who died for me so I might have everlasting life, and I ask that You forgive my sins, come into my heart, and save me. I ask this humbly in the name of Your Son, Jesus Christ.'"

Chloe, with eyes wet from tears that took her by surprise, lowered her head and sighed deeply.

"Please, Jesus, what he said . . . please help me. What that preacher said . . . and please save me."

Music burst forth from the television, startling Chloe so that she raised her head and looked. The camera lens was set on a woman in a purple robe at the podium who was blaring forth a beautiful song, one Chloe had never before heard, something about "amazing grace." She watched, captivated, until the singer was finished, not even noticing as the rest of the papers the police officer had given her slipped from the side of the bed where she laid them and drifted lightly to the floor.

She felt . . . at peace.

"God loves you," the man said. Chloe smiled.

She looked out the window, at the gray sky, the gray tree trunks, the gray that was the day, but rather than see the gray, she saw something else. Dangling from the branches closest to her window were bunches of small green leaves, waving lightly in the wind. Chloe squinted, then laughed in surprise. They were in the shape of hearts.

Dozens of leaves, even hundreds of leaves, all in the shape of hearts. How had she missed seeing that earlier? Chloe must have looked out that window 100 times in the last weeks in the hospital. But until that minute, all she noticed were trees and grass and sky.

The hearts danced as Chloe continued to watch.

"Excuse me—miss?"

A nurse in pink scrubs stood in the doorway, her hair spilling from a white webbed cap. She flipped loudly through papers on her clipboard, pausing as she read. Then with a quick movement, she tucked the board under her arm, strode to Chloe's bedside, and began fiddling with the tubes and knobs. Every few seconds, she would stop and consult something on her board, make a couple notes with a shiny silver pen, then flap the pages down loudly and fiddle with the next tube and knob.

"Are you in pain? What's your pain level?" She kept fiddling as she talked. "Tell me, on the scale of one through ten, with one being no pain and ten the worst, how would you describe your pain?"

With shock, Chloe realized she hadn't felt pain in her body for some time.

"It's weird," Chloe said, lifting her wrist and stroking it gently, carefully, afraid one wrong move might send a jolt of pain through her hand. She looked at the nurse in wonder. "You know, a little while ago, I would've said an eight, maybe even a nine. But right now, I feel nothing."

"No pain?"

"No." Chloe looked at the nurse in disbelief. "No pain."

The nurse resumed her notetaking and Chloe watched with annoyance as she simply tucked the board back under her arm without comment.

"Can I get you another blanket? Another pillow perhaps?"

Chloe shook her head, still baffled at her pain's disappearance, but leery it was lurking in the background somewhere, waiting for a single wrong move to return with a vengeance. She carefully laid her wrist back on the blanket and waited for the nurse to finish.

"Oh, yes, I almost forgot," she said, while pulling a phone-shaped device by the cord from beneath Chloe's hip that served as both a call button for the nurses and a remote control for the television. Absently, she placed it on the side table and worked to untwist the cord. "This was buried underneath you. Were you looking for this?" She pointed it at the TV and lowered the volume, then placed it with a loud smack back on the table. "You don't want to set off the call button in the middle of the night, do you? Or worse, wake yourself up by laying on it and turning on the TV?" She laughed, as Chloe stared.

"Anyhow, like I was saying, I almost forgot," she said, standing and looking down at Chloe. "The victim in the car accident you were in, the gentleman you hit?"

Chloe looked blankly at her. Then, as her words sunk in, she dropped her eyes to her lap and picked uncomfortably at her blanket with her good hand.

"Yes?" Chloe didn't raise her head as she whispered.

"Well, he'd like to come and talk with you, if that's okay."

Horrified, Chloe's head shot up. "Why!"

The nurse gave her a quizzical look, then her eyes turned soft, and she patted Chloe on the shoulder.

"He seems like a nice man," she said, nodding as she spoke. "He wasn't injured; he actually said to tell you he's going to be fine and he just has a couple bruises, but nothing serious."

Chloe chewed her bottom lip furiously as she took in the nurse's words.

"Honestly, I just think he might want to know how you're doing," the nurse said. "When he heard how badly you were injured, he was really upset. He came back to see you once or twice before, but you were out of it, so he didn't stay. He just prayed outside your room door and then left."

Chloe listened in shocked silence.

The nurse leaned in, and Chloe caught a glimpse of something shiny falling from her neck. It was a golden cross, dangling from a delicate golden chain, and Chloe followed it with her eyes as it swayed while the nurse, with a low, gentle voice, said, "I'm not really supposed to tell you this, but really, you were in such bad shape when you got here, we weren't sure you were going to fully recover." She looked into Chloe's eyes. "You must have someone upstairs looking out for you. Your guardian angel was really working overtime to save you."

Chloe, uncomfortable at the nurse's intimacy, pulled back a bit and said the first thing that popped in her mind.

"Yeah, I guess he was taking a coffee break when I got in the accident, though, right?"

Her words came out more bitter and sarcastic than she intended and before she could feel the full shame from the hurt expression she brought to the nurse's face, she quickly added, "But yes, you can tell him he can visit me whenever he likes."

The nurse moved to the door without saying anything. Then she stopped and flipped through her papers again.

"By the way, his name is James Clark." She looked at Chloe with a strange little smile.

"That's *Pastor* James Clark," she said. "He heads up a church a few miles away."

CHAPTER SIX

"Ahh, hello there?"

Chloe's eyes shot to the man in her doorway.

"Umm, hi. Hi there." He took a step toward her bed, then another, and stopped and raised an awkward hand in a half wave. He waited a couple seconds, and when Chloe didn't respond, walked the rest of the space to her bed, cleared his throat, and reached out a hesitant hand.

"I'm James Clark," he said, smiling as he lifted her hand, the one unwrapped by gauze, and held it gently between both of his. "Pastor James Clark, really. Well, Jim. You can call me Jim. My friends do." He placed Chloe's hand back on the bed as he turned his head over his shoulder. Seeing a chair, he dragged it loudly across the floor, positioning it about two feet from Chloe's shoulder. He sat, then got up, repositioned it a couple inches closer, and plopped himself into it again. Chloe watched him cautiously, taking in the glint of humor in his eyes and the light wrinkles of his forehead that seemed to express concern and sympathy, but she only returned his gaze with a barely noticeable uptick of her lip.

Much as she wanted to like him, she didn't want to let down her guard. Not yet, not until she knew why he wanted to visit, at least. The nurses may have all agreed he was a nice man who just wanted to check on Chloe's welfare. But she was suspicious, just the same.

"Or," he went on, leaning bent elbows on her bed railing, "you can call me Pastor Jim if you prefer. Pastor James is good too. It's a bit more formal, but that's fine. Whatever you like. Whichever you prefer." He paused, still not blinking. "Your choice completely."

His voice trailed off but his smile never wavered.

He wasn't anything like Chloe expected. She thought pastors were unsmiling, somber, even angry men who went around and told people they were acting wrong and that they were going to hell. True, she never really knew any pastors, but when the nurses told her about Pastor Clark, her immediate visions were of an old man or at least an older man with grayish hair, with a stern expression who was going to come and lecture her about the evils of drinking alcohol, and perhaps even threaten her with court action. She hadn't been too worried about the court action; after all, she had nothing to really lose in a lawsuit. She was broke.

But she could do without the lecture.

She sat through enough of those with her parents and with police to last a lifetime.

But the man in front of her now was nothing like what she had pictured. This man had light brown hair that wasn't exactly spikey, but it was cut jagged and lay almost messily about his head. He wore a leather jacket, jet-black, beneath which an oddly crisp white shirt collar peeked. His pants were classic tan and sharply pressed, but his shoes, which she had seen as he pulled the chair across the floor, were boots a biker might wear. She wondered whether he was dressed for the sales office or the bar. He dropped his head slightly to remove a pair of bronze-framed glasses from his face and when he did, Chloe saw with a bit of surprise a dark dot on his left ear that she quickly realized was a hole where an earring might fit.

It was his eyes that held her attention, though.

They were deep blue, the deepest blue she ever had seen in eyes, but it wasn't even the color so much as their expression. They gazed unblinking, not in a manner of intimidating, but rather in the way of someone with an intense interest in seeing not just the surface, but beyond. She got the feeling he was skilled at reading people. For a brief moment, staring back into the blue, she wondered if he knew what she was thinking. Then he spoke, and she blinked, embarrassed at her own staring.

"So," he said, running his hands along the railing of her bed and smiling widely, showing a row of perfect teeth save for one in front that angled slightly over another, "what's it going to be?"

Chloe scrunched her nose in confusion.

"What?"

He thumped his chest lightly with an open palm. "What would you like to call me?" He finally blinked and with relief, so did Chloe.

"Oh," she said, trying to remember the options. "I dunno. I guess Jim."

"Jim it is then." He sat back in his chair with a look of satisfaction. "Like I said, that's what my friends call me anyway."

"You're not my friend." Chloe blurted it out before she could catch herself. She didn't meant to sound harsh. "I mean—I meant, I was just trying to say . . ."

His laugh caught her off guard and she scowled.

"What I meant to say is we don't even know each other, so if you'd rather I called you Pastor Jim, I'm fine with that."

"Okay," he said, after regarding her for several quiet seconds with a lopsided grin. "Pastor James it is." His eyes danced, and he clapped his hands with finality. "Now that we've cleared that up." He leaned in close, ignoring Chloe's flinch.

"And you can always call me Jim whenever you feel more comfortable."

Chloe nodded politely, unsure what to say. She glanced quickly at his arms, his face and neck, his torso, checking for any signs of injuries or brokenness. Her cheeks warmed when she saw he was watching her.

He raised his right hand in the air.

"This was my only injury," he said, grinning as he turned his wrist first to the left and then to the right. "See that?" Chloe looked closely at the area of bone where his finger pointed. She didn't want to let on she didn't see anything, so she nodded a few times and pursed her lips in sympathy. His grin grew wider and he dropped his hand back to his side.

"Yeah, it's hard to see. There's still a bruise there if you squint hard enough."

"I guess I can't squint hard enough," she said, looking up in surprise as he laughed.

"No, I suppose it's nothing compared to your injuries. Tell me, are you still in pain?"

Chloe nodded, keeping her eyes averted from his. After all, it was her own fault. She didn't expect sympathy and she didn't want him to think she was seeking it.

"I'm so sorry to hear that. You know, my entire congregation has been praying for you—first, that you survived and then, after we knew you were going to survive, that you heal quickly. But I think maybe we could have done better praying specifically for God to lessen your pain." He reached out his hand and patted her reassuringly on the shoulder. Chloe, shocked at his words, searched his face. When she realized he wasn't mocking, she snapped her lips together tight in more shock.

"Maybe," he said softly, "maybe we could try right now."

Try what? Chloe gave him a quizzical look.

"Praying," he said. "Maybe we could try praying specifically that God lessen your pain." When she still lay silent, he tried again. "I mean now. Maybe you and I could pray together. Would you like that?"

Chloe nodded dumbly. She didn't know what else to do.

She tried to pull herself higher in the bed but moved too fast and her leg twisted in its cast. Instinctively, she grabbed at her leg with her hands, sending a hot flame of pain through her wrapped wrist.

"Owww!" She cursed, then cursed again, as pain shot up her back, alongside her hip, down her leg, and through her wrist. She had a new crick in her neck and as she tried to calm the other throbbing parts of her body by gently rubbing with her one good hand on the areas she could reach, the muscle by her shoulder cricked and creaked and stretched uncomfortably. She cursed again.

She glanced at his face, expecting to see shock and outrage and maybe even anger. But his face displayed none of those things. He was laughing—and not just any old laugh. He was laughing so hard the rail he grasped with one hand was actually shaking her bed. Her eyes widened in disbelief and for a few short seconds, she forgot about her throbbing wrist. He coughed and squeezed fingers from a cupped hand over his mouth as if trying to wipe away his laughter or at the least conceal it.

"Aren't you supposed to be a pastor?" She couldn't keep the astonishment from her tone.

He swallowed hard and wiped one eye with the point of his finger. His face was flushed and before he spoke, he flashed a conspiratorial wink and leaned in close, slightly bending an open hand along the side of his mouth as if about to share a secret.

"I'm not that kind of pastor," he said, in a loud whisper. Then he sat back straight and reached out both arms, laying them on top of her arm. His expression turned serious and he gazed into her eyes.

"Now how about we try that prayer." It was more statement than question. "Seems like you could really use it about now."

Chloe couldn't help but smile.

"Okay."

He lowered his head. Chloe did too, then shut her eyes, peeking now and again as if he weren't real and might disappear if she let her lids stay closed for too long.

"Dear Father in heaven, thank You so much for Your sovereign rule and Your never-changing ways. Thank You for being the rock that cannot be moved. Thank You for granting me such great medical care from the doctors and nurses at this hospital—" At that, Chloe flicked open her eyes to search his face for hidden meaning. Finding none, she pressed her lids together once again.

"—and for allowing me to come from the accident unscathed—for allowing me to come out of this accident whole and healthy and with barely a scratch. And Father, I know that while this may have been an accident to us, for You, it was not the least bit of a surprise, and You knew before it ever took place that it was going to take place.

"I know too, Father," he went on, "that whatever the evil one means for wickedness, You can use for good. And I know You will use this accident for the good of me, as well as for the good of Chloe, all so in the end, You are glorified."

Chloe peeled open her eyes, confused by his words and wondering how good could come of a car accident. But he wasn't finished and she didn't want to interrupt, so she shut them tight as he kept on praying.

"But Father, on the way toward Your glorification, we ask a special request that You might lessen Chloe's pain. She is hurt and healing, both in body and spirit, and if it's in Your will, Father, we pray You might grant her speedy recovery. And whatever other pains Chloe might be suffering at this moment—whether physical, from this accident; whether spiritual or mental or pains of the heart—we ask You to heal her. Heal her from her past, heal her from her present, heal her from whatever might come in the future You already see, but we don't know. And please give her the peace that surpasses all understanding as You do this healing for her. In the name of Jesus Christ, Your Son, our glorious Savior, we pray. Amen."

He raised his head and looked at Chloe, letting his hands fall back to his lap.

"Umm." She lay awkwardly, not sure how to respond. Finally, she turned her head toward his and said, "That was nice." But her heart was so warm she reached up and touched her chest with her fingertips, to see if she were imagining. She pulled her fingers away and rubbed them lightly together, feeling their heat too.

"I've never, umm." She cleared her throat and tried again. "I've never had anyone pray for me before."

"Never?"

She shook her head.

He reached over and patted her hand, then held it in his own.

"Anytime you need prayer, all you have to do is ask," he said. "And guess what's great about prayer?" He waited until she focused her eyes on his. He smiled, then shrugged. "You don't have to wait for someone to pray to God for you. You can talk to God yourself. And if you listen hard enough, you'll find—He answers."

Once again, Chloe couldn't think how to respond.

"I'm really tired," she finally said, letting her head drop against her pillow and reaching up to rub her eye.

He stood abruptly, the metal legs of the chair scraping painfully loud against the flooring.

"Of course," he said briskly. "You need your sleep. I'll let you get some rest and . . ." He trailed off, looking over his shoulder as he stepped toward the doorway.

"And I'll come visit you again?"

He didn't wait for her to answer, but reached into the inside of his jacket, pulled something out and dropped it quickly next to her on the bed.

"I'll come back tomorrow."

Chloe reached for what he dropped and when she lifted her head again, he was gone. She looked at the small white card in her hand and turned it to the light to read. It was a business card. On one side, she read, "James Clark. Pastor, Friendship Christian Church. Jesus Welcomes All."

Then she turned it over and the short message made her suck in sharply. In large black letters, the words, GOD LOVES YOU.

CHAPTER SEVEN

Chloe shot the nurse a look of panic.

"Did you hear me, honey?"

Chloe sighed, then nodded.

"Yeah, I heard you." Chloe looked sadly at the cast on her leg and the brace around her wrist.

"We just can't discharge you without having someone pick you up," the nurse repeated, tapping her pen on her clipboard for emphasis. "You have a friend? Family member? Even a neighbor?" She consulted her paperwork again. "I just don't see anyone listed here as your emergency contact."

"Can't I just call a taxi?" Chloe already knew the answer. The night nurse explained the discharge process.

"No. The hospital policy won't allow that."

Chloe bit her bottom lip nervously, running down her list of friends in her mind. Most, she knew, were probably recovering from hangovers. Even if they weren't, Chloe doubted their willingness to drive her home from the hospital.

If I even have a home to go to, she thought, despondently. She had been already late on her rent at the time of her accident.

CHLOE

The nurse tapped impatiently. Chloe pushed away the visions of her belongings tossed on the front yard of her home, not even boxed, and flashed the woman a smile.

"How about I get back to you on that? If you give me a few minutes, I can call and see who's available," she said as cheerily as she could.

"Okay, honey," the nurse said, shutting her clipboard with a loud click. "But be sure and let me know who's coming for you. I have to have their contact information for this." She tapped her board. "They won't let you out of here unless you have someone to pick you up. Not in your condition."

"Until they find out I have no money anyway," Chloe said jokingly. But the nurse pretended not to hear.

Alone again, Chloe turned to the window and watched as the rain and wind whipped at the trees, rattling the branches into mad little dances. She stared gloomily, counting first the branches then the tips of the branches, then the numbers of times the branches clacked together. The leaves of hearts she had seen weeks ago were now indiscernible, roiled by the pounding of rainwater into tight little balls. *It is a good day for a rainstorm*, she thought.

Two weeks ago, she couldn't wait to get out of the hospital. Now, faced with actual discharge, faced with the realities of what that discharge meant, she wished she could stay another month. Or longer.

It wasn't entirely a bad thing to have someone take care of you, she decided, running her hand down the length of her leg cast and holding it, and thinking of her empty refrigerator and baskets of dirty laundry. An image of herself hopping unsteadily on one leg as she tried to carry laundry made her groan. The realization she didn't have a car to drive to the laundromat made her groan again. Frustrated, she counted in her mind all the things she would not be able to do any longer. Tears welled and her shoulders sagged.

She looked at the dark television set, as if expecting some words of comfort and guidance to come. Then she saw the remote on the table next to her and shook her head sadly.

"God," she finally said, in as low a voice as possible. She paused to look at the door. After waiting a few seconds, she began again. "God, I don't really know if You're listening, or how to do this. But if You are listening, I could really use some help." She paused, listening . . . for what, she wasn't sure.

After a full minute of sitting in tense then embarrassed silence, she shrugged and reached for the remote. Through her watery vision, she misjudged the distance and knocked it on the floor. As she bent to retrieve it by the cord, she noticed something else had fallen, as well.

It was the card left by Pastor James, flipped to the side that read GOD LOVES YOU in all caps, and she carefully leaned over to pick it up. She had just turned it to look at the side with the pastor's name and contact information, when the nurse burst into the room.

"Do you have a pick-up person yet, Chloe?" Her voice was sharp and she was hurriedly trying to push her stray hairs back into her bun. When they wouldn't stay, she finally reached up and yanked hard at the top of her head, and then spent several seconds pushing the tangled mass that fell back from her face using both hands. Chloe watched with interest, noting the dark stain on the front of the nurse's top that wasn't there an hour ago.

"Well?"

Chloe looked at the card in her hand, then back at the frazzled nurse, and smiled.

"Yes. I do," she said.

The nurse pulled her clipboard from beneath her armpit and flipped open the pages. Pen in hand, she stood waiting. "Name."

"James Clark." Chloe paused for the nurse to write. "Pastor James Clark. I have to call him now."

The nurse flashed her a look of annoyance, but before she could say anything, Chloe blurted, "He was busy. They said to call back."

That was a lie, of course. But it got the nurse to leave. Chloe took a deep breath and picked up the phone and began dialing very slowly.

Chloe eased herself out of the wheelchair and with a curt "I got it," she pushed away the nurse's arm and hopped as best she could toward the gray leather seat.

She misjudged the height and was about to fall to the pavement, when Pastor James reached out and steadied her around the waist with both hands.

"That's why we tell patients to stay in the wheelchair and let us get them in the car," the nurse said, a bit snobbishly.

Chloe spun her head toward her and was about to say something, then saw Pastor James's expression and let the thought die on her lips. She settled instead for staring icily at the woman as she wheeled the chair back into the hospital.

"We want to thank you so much for your help," Pastor James called after her, smiling broadly even though she didn't see it. She turned at the door, though, and with first a frosty glare at Chloe, then a wide smile at the pastor, she waved. Chloe scowled.

"You see that look she gave me?" she asked, after Pastor James hopped into the cab beside her and shifted into drive.

"I mean, talk about rude." Chloe stared hard out her window, hoping for one more look at the offending nurse. She flipped her face to him quickly, though, after she heard him laughing.

"You mean her or you?"

Now it was his time to be on the receiving end of Chloe's glare. To her surprise, he started humming softly, and after a few seconds, defeated, she turned to the window again.

"Well now, that's over with, isn't it?" He glanced her way, and chuckled.

"What's so funny?"

"Oh, I don't know," he said, steering around the rotary to exit the hospital parking lot. "I'm just wondering what it was you were thinking of saying to that nurse back there— you know, right before I helped you in the truck and shut the door on you so you wouldn't say something you regretted?"

Chloe pursed her lips but kept her eyes focused at the windshield.

"I was just going to thank her for her help," she said coolly.

She bit her lip to keep from joining his laughter and instead, ran fingers along the leather of her seat, tapping lightly on the gleam of the dashboard.

"Nice truck."

It was. The seats were soft and supple, real leather, and unlike any seats in any car she had ever before ridden. The black dashboard glittered, and try as she might, Chloe couldn't see dust anywhere, not even in the tight angled space that met the windshield. The windows sparkled, front and sides, and the carpets appeared so freshly vacuumed that Chloe figured the truck was either brand-new or nobody ever rode in it without first removing shoes. For the life of her, Chloe couldn't remember ever riding in a vehicle that didn't stink of old cigarette smoke and trash and she sniffed appreciatively, breathing in a mix of leather and lemon.

She reached for the stereo and ran her finger along the push buttons. They were clean, too, and she bet not one of them was in a stuck position because someone in a drunken state pushed too hard. Curious about his choice in music, she hit the pre-sets and smiled as one country song after another blared.

Figures, she thought. She hated country.

"It's not mine," he said.

She looked at him in surprise and dropped her hand back to her lap.

"Oh."

"It's borrowed," he said with a shrug. He shot her a side-wise glance, and Chloe caught the slight smile that sprung to his lips.

"Somebody totaled my car in a crash." Chloe's face turned white and her heart began to beat hard, but he just laughed. He reached over with his hand and gently pushed her on the shoulder.

"Good thing for insurance, right?" She nodded, but stammered, searching awkwardly for the right words, the proper way to apologize.

"Hey. I'm sorry. I'm truly only joking around," he said, waving his hand in the air. He waited until she smiled in return. "I just couldn't resist, that's all. But I promise—no more jokes." They rode several minutes in silence.

Then he flicked at the steering wheel, and let loose a long sigh.

"But you have to admit, this really is a nice ride, right? It's a real upgrade from what I had. And when you called, I was just going to take the church van to pick you up, but one of my flock happened to be in my office and overheard enough to get the gist of what was going on and offered his truck. What could I say?" He swept his right hand along the dashboard as if touching an item of beauty, then pointed his fingers at the wood trim, the GPS, the security system. "This is a much nicer drive than the church van, trust me." He stopped at an intersection, nodded at a nearby McDonald's and asked, "How about a cup of coffee or something to eat?"

Chloe shook her head.

"But if you want to go," she said quickly, before they passed, "go ahead. I don't mind at all."

"Nope. Just thought you might be hungry after all that hospital food, that's all." He hit the gas and Chloe was thrown hard against the back of her seat. She delicately repositioned her wrist and checked to see if the brace was fastened properly.

"Okay, then. Let's get you home."

She felt her heart drop at the thought of her home, and she let out a little "oh." Her face grew hot as she felt his glances.

"Something wrong?"

Chloe nodded, but she didn't trust herself to speak. Her leg was starting to throb and the more she thought of navigating her dirty home on crutches for the next few weeks, the more her leg throbbed. And that was if she even had a home, she thought, her chest growing tight.

Her good leg was already tiring from bracing her body to keep her cast from being jarred as they bounced around curves. She couldn't imagine how tired she would be crutching to the bathroom, hopping around the bedroom, leaning on crutches as she cooked. She couldn't imagine what would happen if, as the doctor warned, she put too much pressure on her wrist and reinjured it. What if she snapped the bone? She shivered at the thought. She didn't have a wheelchair, and doubted she could afford one.

She fought off tears, not daring to blink. She caught sight of herself in the rearview mirror, though—a sad-eyed, red-eyed, wide-eyed girl. A hot drop fell, then another, and when she reached up quickly to wipe them away, a third fell right into her lap.

She stole a glance at Pastor James. His eyes were fixed on the road in front, but something about his expression told her he saw her tears.

"I guess my leg is starting to hurt a bit," she finally said, casting a woeful look at her cast.

He didn't answer; just kept driving. Chloe, twisting inwardly in embarrassment at the silence, cursed herself for her stupidity. Suddenly, she couldn't wait to get home and get out of the truck.

"Matthew 7:7. Ask and it shall be given you. Seek and ye shall find. Knock and it shall be opened unto you."

His words startled her and she scrunched her face in confusion.

"What?"

"It's in the Bible," he said. "It's a quote from the Bible. The book of Matthew, chapter seven, verse number seven." He glanced at her grimace and smiled. "You've never read that? You've never read the Bible, I take it." She shook her head. Pastor James steered around a tight corner before continuing. "It goes on, you know. It doesn't end there. It goes on to say, 'For every one that asketh receiveth, and he that seeketh findeth, and to him that knocketh, it shall be opened.'"

"Matthew 7:8," he finished, letting the wheel slide smoothly through his hands as he navigated another sharp turn.

Chloe didn't know what to say. She stared out the windshield and chewed lightly on her bottom lip, listening politely as Pastor James talked about some guy named Matthew, and wondering if "knocketh" meant the same as "knock."

"Of course, most people take that out of context to use for their own selfish reasons," Pastor James said. "They think it's magic—like God's their personal magic genie and all they have to do is call on that passage to get what they want." He sniffed and peered at a passing sign. "They'd be wrong, of course," he said flatly, peering at Chloe over the top of his glasses and looking so much like an old man she stifled a laugh.

"But I just say it now for this reason: You obviously have a question, but are afraid to ask. But if you don't asketh, you can't receiveth."

Chloe gave him a look of surprise.

"I don't have a question," she said.

"No?" He flashed her a crooked smile.

"No." She thought for a moment. "I mean," she started, then paused. "I mean, no, I don't have anything to ask. Why? What do you mean? Do you have something to ask me?"

She was starting to feel very bewildered.

"I think maybe," he started to say, then stopped as he steered to the side of the road. He let the engine idle, but turned to her. "I think maybe there's something you'd like to ask, but don't know how to go about it because you're not used to asking people for help." She reddened under his stare. "Or maybe it's that you're not used to asking people for help with spiritual matters."

She thought hard on his words. An image of him praying over her in the hospital sprang to mind, and immediately, she tried to shake it away. But it stubbornly stayed until finally, perplexed at the seeming randomness of the vision, she tapped lightly at her cast.

"Well," she said shyly, holding her eyes fast on the truck seat, "I was just thinking that maybe you could do that thing you did at the hospital that made my pain in the wrist go away." She held her breath and quickly added, "Only for my leg this time."

She squirmed, feeling immediately silly.

"Thing?" He chuckled. "You mean prayer?"

"Well, yeah," she said, avoiding his gaze. "Prayer. I mean." She stopped, her discomfort rising. Her embarrassment turned to stabs of anger, and she was just about to tell him to forget it when he shifted in his seat to face her.

"Of course. Let's pray now."

He took her one good hand in his, and gently touched her other, laying his fingers across the brace, then bowed his head. She shut her eyes tight and listened, breathing in as quietly as she could, then releasing with slow, sporadic puffs, afraid even that small sound or movement might break the spell of his prayer.

He finished and patted her hands and she looked up in surprise.

"Oh, we're done?"

"You know," he said laughing, sliding back to the driver's wheel and flipping his left turn signal to ease into the road, "that's a dangerous thing to say to a pastor." She looked at him quizzically. "Because the joke is we like to talk so much."

"Ohh," she said. "I get it."

She didn't know what else to say, so she watched the clouds through the window and made imaginary animals out of the fluffy shapes. *That one looks like a lizard*, she thought. *That one, an elephant. There—right there is a mushroom with a frog on it*, she thought, shaking her head at the strangeness of the shapes. *And right there—that's a heart.* She tilted her head toward the windshield, peering straight to the sky. The heart shape was unmistakable, just as unmistakable as the heart leaves had been outside her hospital window.

"We're here," he said.

Chloe looked across the lot to a building with a large cross on top of it.

"Church?" She read the sign: Friendship Christian Church. "What the—" the words were out of her mouth before she could stop them, and chagrined, she threw her hand over her mouth.

Pastor James shot her a reproachful look.

"Watch your language, now. We're about to enter a house of God."

"Sorry." She felt her cheeks warm and she stared at her lap.

"For there is not a word in my tongue, but, lo, O Lord, you know it altogether."

Chloe furrowed her brows.

"From Psalm 139," he said.

She shot him a look of reproach. "Do you always do that?" When he laughed, she only scowled deeper. "Do you have to do that?"

"Well, I am a preacher, you know," he said, jumping from his seat and slamming the door. A few seconds later, he was at Chloe's door, pulling it wide and helping her with her crutches.

"Okay," Pastor James said, guiding her toward the front door. "I know you probably want to get home and rest." He shot a dubious look at the cast on her leg. "And I know you're in pain." Chloe gritted her teeth tightly, concentrating on hobbling without falling and on keeping her wrist as straight as possible on the crutch handle. "But I thought we could just stop in here first. I have a couple things I need to take care of and then we could chat for a few minutes, if you want."

Chloe gave him a suspicious look, but said nothing. She crutched gingerly past the door he held open, into the front entrance of the church. She surveyed the deep red carpet, the wood paneling, cream white paint, the dozens of black-and-white framed photographs lining the wall, leading the eyes like horizontal stepping stones down a corridor ending with a floor-to-ceiling window. Right outside the window was a massive tree with a thick trunk, possibly the thickest trunk Chloe ever saw, and spreading off the truck were dozens and dozens of thick, wavy branches weighted with beautifully sprouting foliage. Then something caught her attention and she leaned forward in rapt attention.

Bobbing gently in the breeze were leaves in the shape of hearts.

As if on cue, her heart warmed. First, the heart cloud. Now the heart leaves. Chloe smiled to herself, fighting off the urge to share her discovery with Pastor James.

"Okay," she said, turning her head and nodding decisively at him. "That'd be fine."

"Great," he said, walking slowly to match her struggling pace. "My office is over here." He quickly stepped in front of her and twisted the door handle. Finding it locked, he rifled through his pockets until he found the keychain, then the key. "Here we go," he said, swinging the door wide and rushing to clear a seat for Chloe in the padded armchair closest to his desk.

He took her crutches and, searching for a suitable spot, finally leaned them against the wall several feet away. Then he walked to a small fridge at the back of the room, positioned somewhat precariously on a cheap-looking brown table between the bookcases and window ledge, and cracked open its door. "Water? Soda?" He held up a bottle of each and waited for Chloe to answer.

"Umm, sure. I'll have a water. Thanks."

He started to hand it to her and then, as an afterthought, pulled it back and cracked open the cap.

"Here you go." Pastor James walked around the corner of his desk, pushing stacks of papers and notebooks to the side as he moved. He gave her a sheepish grin, grabbing random papers and piling them messily in the upper corner of his desk. "Your call kind of caught me in the middle of dealing with something."

"I see that." Chloe stole a couple peeks at the papers, but he was fussing with them too much for her to read anything.

"Now," he said, plopping into the chair next to her, and folding his fingers across his stomach. "Let's chat about your plans." He scooted a couple inches closer and leaned his elbow on his desk as he scrutinized her face. "How many times did we talk at the hospital—five? Six?"

Chloe mentally counted.

"I think you came a total of seven times, counting the first day we met."

He nodded. "And during all that time, did I ever ask you about what you were planning to do after you got out of the hospital?"

Chloe thought for a moment, then shook her head. They had talked a little about her injuries, her waitress job, her family, quite a bit about hospital food, which nurse was the nicest, and how doctors always seemed so sure about their diagnoses, even when they were wrong—even when they were wrong more than once. She wrinkled her nose and remembered their conversations of God—about the Bible and why she should read it every day, and why it was best to start with John, not Romans or Revelation, and how Jesus and the cross were really the foundations of Christianity. Mostly, those conversations were one-sided; Pastor James did most of the talking, and Chloe did most of the puzzled listening. Every now and then, though, she asked a question and he would answer, with a straight-forward demeanor, never criticizing, never treating her as if she were stupid. She came close a couple times to telling him about the television preacher and the hearts. She felt awkward even thinking about it, though, so she held her tongue.

"No," Chloe finally said. "We never talked about anything after the hospital."

"I didn't think so," he said, sitting up straight, then stretching and standing, taking a few steps toward his bookcase. He spun back to her suddenly. "So," he said, clapping his hands together as if preparing to announce a great decision.

"Pastor Clark?"

Chloe's head jerked toward the door. A man with very large eyes framed by stark black square glasses stuck his head into the room, shot a blank look at Chloe, and then turned his eyes back to the pastor. Even from the distance of several feet, Chloe could see the whites around his eyes. He looked stressed or maybe distressed. The words of a song she once heard on the radio popped into her mind—something about not firing until you see the whites of their eyes—and without realizing, Chloe started to hum. She felt Pastor James's gaze, and abruptly stopped, clearing her throat and politely folding her braced hand over the other as best she could. She twisted her body back to face the desk and kept her eyes hard on an imaginary dot on the wall.

"Peter." James's voice was a mix of concern and annoyance and Chloe wondered at his tone, surprised at the idea of a pastor being impatient with anyone. He returned to his chair.

"Yes, I'm so sorry to interrupt, Pastor. But there's a problem with the—" he paused, glancing pointedly at Chloe. He leaned his head in, as if to whisper. But his voice grew curiously louder, not quieter, and Chloe nearly laughed. "With the gardeners."

"With the—gardeners." Pastor James's tone was flat, and he waited for further explanation. But Peter clamped his lips tight and as the moments passed into seconds and nobody spoke, Chloe began to feel more and more like an intruder. She wished the pastor hadn't put her crutches so far away, and she was about to ask him to get them for her, so she could make an excuse to leave, when he spoke.

"Okay," Pastor James said, sighing deeply while standing and pushing his chair back noisily. The legs grated on the floor and Chloe winced at the squeak. "Apparently, there's a problem with the gardeners that needs my immediate attention. Will you be all right alone for a few minutes?" His tone was level and he didn't say anything that gave indication he was annoyed, but Chloe, watching him leave, had the distinct impression he didn't appreciate the interruption.

"Oh, take your time," she said, still astonished at the notion of a pastor feeling bothered by someone seeking assistance.

"Take your time," she said again, her voice trailing as they shut the door behind them.

She spent the next several minutes examining his office in greater detail, taking note of the stacks and stacks of books spilling off the shelves onto the floor; the colorful array of candles, most half burnt, on the table that held the refrigerator; the table she now noticed was balanced with the help of a folded piece of paper or cardboard—she couldn't tell which—shoved beneath one of the front legs; the printer and fax machine clumsily shoved on top of what looked like an antique bureau; and on top of the printer sat a large, thick stack of papers. She glanced again at the messy pile in front of her on top of his desk, and sighed impatiently. She was starting to grow bored.

Her leg was giving her pain, so she shifted to redistribute the weight. When that didn't work, she pulled herself to her feet and stood on one foot, balancing herself by holding the arm of her chair. The blood shifted in her body enough that she found relief from her leg pain. She eyed her crutches and mentally calculated steps.

Sixteen, she sighed. *Too many.* Then a thought occurred and she plopped back into her chair and using her good leg, slowly inched across the floor. When she arrived at her crutches, she stood again and carefully, placed them under her armpits, taking great care to position her healing wrist. Slowly, she took a hop, then reached with her unhurt hand to the arm on the chair and gently pulled. It moved a few inches forward and she took another hop with her crutches. She progressed that way for several cautious minutes until she was able to return the chair to its spot in front of the pastor's desk.

Sitting once again, she placed her crutches flat on the floor in front of her. Her leg was beginning to hurt again, and she looked about for a distraction, tapping her fingers impatiently on his desk. With a quick glance at the door, she reached and grabbed a couple of the papers he had piled in the corner. Curious, she began to sift through and read.

They were bills—unpaid, by the looks of it.

Bright red "Last Warning" and "past due" messages blared from each page as she shuffled. She noticed a small book with a green leather cover marked in gold lettering "LEDGER" alongside the pile, and reached for it. The more she scanned through it, the more her astonishment grew. There were more empty boxes than she could immediately count and the ones that were filled with numbers, she saw with growing alarm, were totaled incorrectly. Still others were simply crossed out and rewritten so many times, and so messily, it was impossible to decipher which numbers were intended. She groaned out loud.

This is horrible, Chloe thought, shaking her head in amazement and continuing to flip pages. Without thinking, she reached for a red pen peeking from one of the piles on the pastor's desk, and shuffled about for a piece of scrap paper. Finding a yellow pad, she balanced it on her knee and went to work.

"No, no, no, no, oh no," she muttered, her pen slicing along the paper, scratching quickly with each tabulation.

"This here, then this, take away that, that, and that . . ." She bit her lip as she worked, the numbers flying off her mind onto the page as she formed neat columns on the yellow pad to correspond to the pages in the ledger. Hastily, she swept her hand across the pastor's desk, sifting through piles until she found a pencil. She threw the pen down dismissively and began jotting figures right on the pages of the ledger, stacking up numbers like building blocks on the side before hastily grabbing the pen she just threw aside, and transferred them in more permanent ink to the boxes. She worked that way for several minutes, computing in her mind and on the side of the ledger in pencil, then taking up the pen to put the correct numbers into the boxes. She was so engrossed, she forgot her throbbing leg.

She was so engrossed, she didn't hear the pastor as he entered.

"Ahhh . . . can I help you?"

His tone was brusque, almost cold, and Chloe sat up so quickly the yellow pad slid from her lap and dropped to the floor along with a few of the bills. Her face turned red as she followed his eyes as he looked to the "late notice" page at her feet.

"I'm sorry," she said, struggling to reach for the papers. But her cast prevented her from bending properly and she grunted with the effort. Finally, she sat up, leaving the papers in their spot on the floor. She waited for him to pick them up for her, but he stood silent in the doorway, staring. Completely disarmed by his stern expression, Chloe began stammering nervously.

After a minute, and without replying, Pastor James strode to her side and began gathering the bills. Standing, he held out his hand for the ledger that had slipped between Chloe's thigh and the armrest. Chloe stared dumbly, then reached down and, without saying another word, handed it to him.

"Thank you."

The curtness of his voice threw her off guard and she sucked in her breath, uncertain how to respond.

"I'm sorry, I'm really sorry. I didn't mean to snoop around. I mean, I wasn't snooping around, it's just—it's just you had all these papers on your desk and I kinda glanced at them and then I saw they were bills and I kinda picked one up to look at it, and then—" she struggled to sit up in her chair, but it was hard to straighten while keeping half her body still. Pain surged through her leg and she bit back a moan. He looked down at her with darkened eyes, his hands in tight little fists as he gripped the papers.

"And then," he said, beckoning one fist of papers toward her, prompting her to finish her sentence.

She took in the tightness of his neck muscles and the grim expression on his face and shrugged her shoulders in defeat.

"And then nothing," she said quietly.

She turned her attention to the window, watching as a bird hopped along the ground, wondering what was to happen next. Several moments of silence passed and then Pastor James sat at his desk, shuffled the stack of bills in his hands, and tapped the bottoms loudly against his desk. Once they were all in line, he slowly, deliberately set them neatly within a bin marked "In Box," then carefully made sure all the corners of the pages were tucked within the plastic borders. He leaned back in his chair, crossed his arms over his chest, and regarded Chloe dispassionately for several long, uncomfortable moments.

Something about his demeanor, whether real or imagined, drew an image in Chloe's mind of her father, in the minutes before he exploded with drunken anger. She looked away anxiously and tried to convince herself her rising alarm was needless. But after glancing once more to his frosty expression, she grabbed for her crutches and struggled to a standing position.

"Could I use your bathroom please?" It was more statement than question, and as she spoke, she was already moving toward the door. She paused, with her hand on the doorknob.

"Maybe you could tell me where it is?" Chloe tried to match his brusque tone, to let him know he wasn't intimidating her; more than that, to let him know she didn't care one way or the other about his anger. But her voice came out squeaky, and she inwardly cursed. She cleared her throat as quietly as she could, hoping he hadn't noticed.

Pastor James stood and almost automatically took a couple steps toward Chloe, as if to help with the door. But she turned her back and as he gave directions, flung open the door and, with difficulty, hopped a couple steps. She hoped she wouldn't fall, at least until she was out of his sight.

"It's to the right," he called. "You go out of here, take a right, and it's about five doors down, by the water fountain."

She was already down the hallway.

"Thanks," she muttered, not bothering to look back at him.

She crutched a few feet, listening for the sound of a closing door. When she heard the tell-tale click, she crutched faster, past several offices, a door marked "Men's Room," then another marked "Women's Room." Instead of going in, she followed the yellow arrows mounted on the ceilings that pointed the way to the exit.

She had no plan about where she was going. She just knew she wasn't returning to the pastor's office. *He can take his angry looks and shove 'em,* she thought.

She was just feet from the glass door leading to the outside world when the rubber tip of her left crutch caught on the carpet and she stumbled. She quickly tried to catch herself, but her body spun and then her crutches jammed crookedly beneath her arms. With a cry of pain and frustration, she crumpled to the floor. She lay there, moaning and cursing, watching as strange face after face peered down at her.

"Are you all right?"

"Ma'am, are you okay?"

"Oh my good Lord, let me help you."

Humiliated, Chloe lay there helpless. Then a face she recognized leaned over her.

"My God, Chloe, are you all right?"

Reluctantly, Chloe looked into Pastor James's eyes, expecting more of the same icy glares from a few minutes ago. But his eyes were blue, soft blue, and as Chloe stared, they almost seemed to turn green. She sighed with relief and embarrassment. Then she recalled the snarky way he told her "thank you," after she handed him the ledger, and stubbornness gripped her heart.

"I'm fine," she said, lifting her chin as she answered him through clenched teeth. She waved away his hands and instead, grabbed the arm of a woman who was holding it out, waiting for Chloe to take it. Slowly, she pulled herself to a sitting position.

"You don't sound it."

He leaned in close to her ear.

"And cursing like a sailor at the top of your voice doesn't make anyone believe it either," he said softly.

"What?" She feigned innocence. But she could tell by the shocked looks on a few of the women's faces who surrounded her that they had heard.

Oh well, she thought, callously. *They'll get over it.*

"Oh well," she said to the pastor, flashing a tight little smile and shrugging. She purposely reached around him for the outstretched hands of two other men, who then helped her to her feet and balanced her while she finagled the crutches beneath her arms.

James laughed quietly and Chloe scowled.

"Okay, I get it," he said, patting her lightly. He turned his head toward the gathering and raised his voice. "I think we can all go about our business now. Then you for your help, but I think we can all just go back to our offices and get our work done." Chloe watched them walk off, glad to no longer be the center of their attention.

"Are you able to crutch about, or do you need to rest?"

"I can crutch," she said as blithely as she could manage through the pulses of pain in her leg and back. She turned to the glass door again, as if getting ready to go.

"No!" His voice surprised her with its loudness and she stopped and looked at him. He cleared his throat and looked down for a second. "I mean, wait. Where are you going?" He searched her face for clues. "Where were you going? The bathroom is back there." Chloe looked in the direction of his pointed finger, but just shrugged in reply.

"Look," he said, spreading his arms and raising his hands, palms up. "I was actually waiting for you to come back to the office so I could apologize. And then you were taking a while so I thought I'd peek my head out to see if you were on your way. And then I heard—"

He paused, as if carefully considering his next words.

"And then I heard your sailors' act and saw everybody around you and figured you fell. So I came running too."

Chloe stood silent, still refusing to smile. He cleared his throat and started again.

"Anyway, like I said, I wanted to apologize to you for the way I treated you . . ." His voice trailed off and he sighed. "Look, can we just go back to my office for a few minutes? Can we just do that, please?" His eyes flashed blue-green and he stepped toward her, reaching for her shoulder. "Can we just talk in private for a minute? I promise, if you don't like what I have to say, if you want to leave right after, I'll help you in the truck and drive you wherever you want to go. I just want to chat for a couple minutes." He waved a hand around the hallway. "Without listening ears, that is."

Chloe finally spoke.

"What do you mean you were about to apologize?"

He smiled, catching her softening demeanor.

"Yes. It's a good apology," he said, steadying her on her crutches. "But tell me," he went on, his eyebrows raised as he fixed her with a look of wonderment, "where were you headed?"

Chloe snorted. "Out," she said.

He chuckled as they made their way back to his office, and once inside, resettled in their chairs, he regarded her in silence for several seconds. She stared right back, waiting for him to speak first.

"So tell me," he finally said, still scrutinizing her face, "where did you learn to do all that math?"

Chloe's mind flashed to her youth, to the face of a teacher she hadn't thought about in years, to the image of a silver keychain she had long ago forgotten. But she said nothing. She didn't quite know what to say. Pastor James gave her a quick glance.

"I have a proposition for you, if you're interested."

CHAPTER EIGHT

Chloe raised her eyebrows and waited. It wasn't what she expected him to say. He shifted in his seat and leaned forward.

"But before I talk about that, before I tell you what my proposition is, I want to make sure you know how sorry I am for the way I treated you."

He gazed at her so intensely she looked away.

"I'm serious, Chloe. I'm very sorry. I had no right to treat you like that. I was upset about what I stepped outside the office to discuss with Peter, and other members in the church—something that's going to cost the church a great deal of money—and then when I came back to my office and saw all those unpaid bills on the floor, I just snapped." He sighed, then continued. "Honestly, it wasn't even you looking at the bills so much as it was seeing the red 'late notice' message on the floor, right after learning about the big expense the church is going to face."

He sighed again and pressed his palms together. "Well, all I can say is I'm sorry. I'm really sorry about speaking to you that way, and I hope you can forgive me and listen to what I wanted to talk to you about with an open mind. Can you?"

Her mind spun but she still said nothing. She was so unaccustomed to receiving apologies, especially noticeably genuine ones, she was too taken aback to speak. Finally, she nodded, and with a loud "good," Pastor James cleared his throat and slapped his hands on his thighs.

"Okay then," he said, briskly. "Moving on." His voice grew animated as he picked up the green book marked "LEDGER" and started flipping through pages.

"Look," he said, pointing here, then there, then there again. "Look what you did. Here." He pointed to a set of boxes, filled with figures. "And here." He spun the book around so she could see the page. "And again, here."

Chloe's eyes followed his finger as he swept across page after page, tracing lightly over now balanced credit and debit columns, and tapping again and again at the pencil scratches and notations she dotted along the margins.

"How did you do that?" His look of admiration and wonder embarrassed Chloe and she looked away, hiding from him the glitter of her eyes as she fought to quiet the joyful thumping in her chest. It had been a long time since she won praise from anybody, about anything, and she didn't quite know how to react.

"No, I'm serious," he said. "I'd really like to know how you did that. Where did you learn all that?"

She thought long and hard before answering. "I guess I've always been good at math," she finally said evenly.

He stared for several seconds.

"You have a gift."

Inexplicably, Chloe felt tears spring to her eyes and she quickly rubbed at them, feigning a sudden and intense itch. If he knew she was wiping tears, he didn't let on.

"I'd like to have you put that gift to work for the church." He spoke slowly, letting the words sink in and watching her face for reaction. "If you're willing." She still didn't speak and he tried again, this time, light-hearted in tone. "That is, if you've forgiven me."

His smile faded as she stared back without expression.

"So," he said, creaking his chair loudly as he shifted and leaned forward, "what I'd really like to do is offer you a job."

"What?" Chloe couldn't keep the shock from her voice.

"I've been struggling for some time to find someone to take care of the books, and the bills, and accounting for the church. It's been kind of difficult to hire somebody who is willing to work for the only salary we can offer—and it's pretty low," he said, pausing to look pointedly at Chloe.

"But I think God has finally brought me somebody."

"What?" It was all she could think to say.

"You. It's you."

Chloe pursed her lips to keep from saying, "what,'" once more, then chewed furiously on the inside of her cheek as she mulled his words.

"What do you mean?" she finally asked.

"It's really very simple," he said, getting up and pacing a few steps, before leaning his body against the edge of his desk. "I need someone who can do the church books, somebody who's good at math. You need some help getting back on your feet—and not just physically." He paused, watching her face for response.

"I can't pay a lot. Especially now," he said, waving his hand toward the door of his office as if reminding her about the earlier interruption with Peter. "But I do have something else besides money I could offer the right candidate." He paused again and smiled at Chloe. "Room and board. For free."

At that, Chloe's head shot up and her mouth opened in the shape of a small "o." She nodded, waiting for him to continue.

"It's like this," he said. "If you did the accounting and bills for the church, then you could stay here while you heal from your injuries. I mean, how were you going to get around at home and alone on crutches, anyway?"

Chloe nodded vigorously, amazed he wondered at the same issue that had worried her for weeks.

"There's an empty room in the back of the church you could stay in—it has its own private bathroom, a refrigerator, it's like a one-room apartment, really," he said. "There's no stove, but the kitchen's right down the hallway and you can use it any time. It even has a working TV. You could stay there as part of payment for your services to the church."

He straightened and started pacing again.

"Of course, you'd still get a paycheck for doing the books, but it would be really low. Very low in fact. Barely above minimum wage right now," he said, spinning toward her and raising a finger in the air. "But there'd be no rent, no electric or water bills, no cable charges, and actually, I could even throw in some free groceries each week, until you're able to get out and about and get to the store to buy your own, anyway. So. What do you think?" He sat back at the edge of the desk and tapped his fingers impatiently.

"Oh, and one more thing," he said. "Whatever doctor's appointments you have, I can make sure you have a ride there and back. I guess you don't have a car anymore, right? Even if you did, you can't drive now, so I'd make sure you get where you need to go."

Chloe sat in stunned silence.

Free room. Free transportation. Free food. And a job—a math job. A job doing something she liked to do. No more waitressing; no more lousy customers. No worries about her destroyed car.

When she finally raised her head to reply, the first thing she saw was not the pastor's face, but rather a small wooden cross hanging on the office wall she had not previously noticed. Beneath was posted a simple message.

"God Loves You."

She sucked her breath in sharply and she gazed at the three words in wonder. Finally, she turned toward the pastor and sighed as she smiled.

"Okay," she said happily. "That sounds great."

He smacked his hands together so loudly, Chloe jumped.

"Fantastic. Let's get you settled." He stood and reached for the green ledger he earlier tossed to the corner of his desk. "We can talk more about this later, if you don't mind," he said cheerfully.

Chloe reached for her crutches and carefully pulled herself to her feet. As she rose, from the corner of her eyes, she caught sight of a colorful display of curly images on the pages of a splayed-open book just to the left of the pastor's mass of bills. Something about the designs drew her to take a second look.

Leaning in, she saw the image was a chapter title written in green cursive letters, designed to look like a vine. Splitting off the vine of letters were blue and yellow dots of color that at first glance, looked like flowers. But as Chloe kept looking and as she peered even closer, she saw with a start the flowers were actually dozens and dozens of tiny, shaped hearts.

"So, what do you think?"

Chloe gazed around the room and smiled.

A bed by the window, dressed in a fluffy white comforter and piled high with pillows, beckoned invitingly, while a nearby chair, with its overstuffed cushion and not one, but two, carefully draped furry throw blankets practically screamed to her to curl up and take a nap.

She crutched over and ran her fingers along the velvety armrest, gently wiping away the trails her touch left on the cloth. A small table with a quaint lamp, next to a pile of books, a beautifully sweet-smelling candle, and a small radio completed the picture of serenity.

She turned to the dresser—*one, two, three*—she counted seven drawers in all; then the matching bureau with mirror, with another four drawers; then curiously, to a large white bowl alongside a patterned blue-and-white pitcher in front of the mirror.

"What's that?" She hobbled to the bureau and ran her finger along the bowl.

"It's a dry sink," Pastor James said, reaching for the pitcher and holding it gingerly in his hands. "It belonged to my grandmother. She gave it to me when I started this church, as a sort of welcoming gift, and said if I ever needed to wash anyone's feet, this was the perfect bowl and pitcher to use."

He put the pitcher back in its place.

"I never told that to anyone before," he said quietly, then glancing almost shyly at Chloe's mirrored reflection.

Chloe said nothing at first, trying to decide if the question on her lips was proper.

"Why would you need to wash someone's feet?" she finally blurted.

He burst out laughing.

"I forgot—you haven't read the Bible, have you?"

Chloe, taken aback by his laughter, only shook her head.

"Well," he said, patting her arm and laughing more, "one day when we have more time, I'll tell you the story." He rubbed his hands together and stepped back. "So," he said again, waving around the room, "what do you think? Will this do?"

Chloe glanced at a door to the side, and then another, then pointed.

"Oh, one is a closet," he said, jumping to open the door, and then reaching for the handle on the other and flinging it wide. "And the other, a bathroom."

Chloe nodded, staring at the white comforter. Her bed at home was made with sheets and cheap blankets from a second-hand store. She hadn't noticed the stain on one of the blankets until she got home, when it was too late to return. No matter how hard she scrubbed, she could never completely remove it. She thought of the many nights under that blanket, twisting it so the stain was at her feet, not near her face.

This white comforter, she thought, *looks brand new.*

"It's great," she finally said, wishing she could stretch on the bed and feel the thick white covers beneath her body.

As if reading her mind, he walked toward the door.

"How about you take some time and rest? Take a nap, do some reading, just sit for a while and relax. We can talk later." He opened the door and paused as if considering. "I have some church business to take care of anyway," he said, cutting her off before she spoke.

"Okay." She had already started moving to the bed. Pastor James smiled and pulled the door as he left.

"I'll come get you for dinner," he said.

Chloe carefully placed her crutches against the side of the bed and climbed on top.

The comforter really was like clouds, and she stretched gratefully, sinking deeply into the white folds. She felt the luxurious clean cotton sheet peeking from beneath the comforter and touched each pillow about her head, not believing there were four. She shut her eyes and breathed deeply, catching the scent of laundry detergent, and smiling happily as she burrowed her head deeper and forgot, for the moment at least, all her worries of the past weeks—of the past years. Her breathing slowed, her thoughts drifted over the events of the day, and her mind filled with happy thoughts of solving mathematical equations.

"Tammy, stop it."

Chloe's eyes shot open at the sudden command.

It was Pastor James's voice, but his tone was tight, and he was speaking loudly from somewhere beyond the door. Then came a woman's voice, and her words made Chloe's breath catch in her throat.

"What if she starts drinking around the children? What if she gets drunk around the children? What if the children in this church walk into the office and see her sitting there with a bottle of beer, or liquor, or whatever it is she drinks—are you still going to defend her then?"

"Tammy, I said stop it!" This time, it was a shout, and Chloe cringed on her bed covers.

She didn't know the pastor could speak that way and she strained to hear more of the conversation. For a second, as bits and pieces floated to her ears, she thought of grabbing her crutches and sticking her head up tight against the door—or even cracking the door. But the act of getting the crutches and crossing the floor would take too much time, and probably blot out half of the words she was catching, so she decided against it. She strained her neck to hear and held her breath as she carefully sat up in bed.

Still, she only made out partial sentences.

"Can't put her up . . . permission . . ." she heard the woman say.

"I'm the . . . in charge . . . can do ..." she heard Pastor James say.

". . . hiring without . . . elders won't . . ." the woman said.

"Tammy, what about . . . without sin . . . stone . . ."

"She could've killed you! Doesn't . . . difference . . . well it does to . . ."

Then there was mumbling, a rather long, quieted mumbling from Pastor James where Chloe couldn't make out any words at all. Then the woman spoke again, and this time, it was very clear.

"If you want to invite an alcoholic into our church family then go right ahead. Just don't expect me to stand by and support you." A second later, a door slammed. Then, it was silent.

Chloe sat ramrod straight in bed, her hands alongside her thighs, both hands gripping tightly at the comforter. She breathed in as quietly as possible, waiting, not daring to move. Several minutes passed and she finally lay back onto the bed. But she held her body rigid, not daring to relax. She didn't catch all of the conversation, but she heard enough to realize they were talking about her. She caught enough to understand not everybody in the church was happy with her arrangement with Pastor James.

Fearfully, she wondered what that meant.

She figured Pastor James might come into the room and explain things for her—reassure her all was well and she was welcome to stay. But minutes passed until nearly an hour passed. Exhausted, Chloe shut her eyes. This time, her thoughts weren't so joyous. She fell into a fitful sleep.

CHLOE

The snow blew across the open field in big billowy gusts and Chloe shivered, watching from the window ledge of her bedroom as a warm fire burned brightly in the background. Somewhere beyond the closed door, her parents were arguing, but she couldn't make out what they were saying. Every now and then, a clatter or clash—the sound of a bottle being dropped, or perhaps hurled—interrupted her thoughts and she would turn, briefly, to look toward the doorway. But the door remained closed and the room stayed dark, except for the glow of the fire, and she knew so long as she could hear their shouts, they weren't coming. It was only in the silence she had to worry.

Then the clatter in the background began to grow louder, more violent, and the voices seemed to get closer, and her heart beat faster and faster, quickening with each shout. She reached a frightened hand to her chest to make sure her heart hadn't burst forth and spilled on to the floor.

She stared hard at the snow, trying to distract her mind from the screams coming closer, ever closer, to the door—yes, they were right at the door now, she was sure of it. Terrified, she began to count falling flakes frantically: *one, two, three, four. One, two, three, four.* There were too many and they were coming too fast. She fought to control the count and screamed for them to slow down, but the flakes didn't listen.

They dropped to the ground faster than she could number them, to the point she only counted five of fifty. And the voice—the voices! They were at the door, so loud she couldn't discern when the pounding started. *One, two, three, four, five.* The bangs on the door sounded like thunder. Just then, a lightning bolt lit the sky, illuminating thousands of uncounted snowflakes hitting the ground. Chloe, terrified, turned to the door just in time to watch it smash open against the wall.

She peered into the abyss on the other side and saw it, a tiny white light, so distant it was almost imperceptible. As she stared, the light grew larger and closer, a soft yellow-white, more glow than beam, and it floated forward, an egg-shaped circle of light against the black background of the abyss. Chloe, transfixed, watched as a shadow stepped from the light, and then as the shadow took shape as a female figure, and then as the female shadow started to drift toward her, surrounded still by the egg-shaped glow; it drifted away from the abyss, toward the comforting warmth of the fireplace. Just as the shadowy female figure reached the edge of darkness, one leg poised to step into the light of Chloe's room, something whisked her back into the blackness of the abyss. Like that, she was sucked away.

"No!" Chloe jumped from the window ledge and lunged to the door. "Come back! Come back! Come back!"

She awoke as she always did from the dream, her body damp with sweat, her cheeks wet with tears.

"Chloe?"

The voice at the door startled her and in her state of partial sleep, Chloe panicked that the shadowy figure of her dream was knocking on her door. Then the voice spoke again and she realized it was Pastor James and she was safe in the comfort of the church room she was given. Then she recalled the angry words of Tammy and began to worry how long she would have the room.

"Chloe," he said, tapping gently on the door, "are you all right? Can I come in?"

She cleared her throat quietly and wiped her forehead with the corner of the comforter, then her cheeks. She fluffed the pillows and tucked the sheet lightly beneath her legs, and with one more quick swipe to her eyes, she answered him.

"Come in." She hoped she hadn't shouted in her sleep.

He flipped the switch on the lamp and light flooded the room. Chloe, surprised at how dark it had grown, wondered how long she slept.

"Are you all right?" he asked. "I heard screaming."

She'd had the dream before. But nobody ever asked her about it because nobody was ever around when she woke from it. She looked at him with wide eyes, rimmed in white, and thought of the woman in the abyss and the pounding on the door.

"Did you have a bad dream?"

She nodded, but kept her head down, waiting for him to laugh it off and tell her it was just a dream. But he didn't.

"How about we go get something to eat and you can tell me about it if you want?" He stepped back and lifted her crutches. "And if you don't want to tell me about it, then we can at least get something to eat," he said, holding them out for her.

Chloe smiled in gratitude as she slid to her feet.

Never would she have considered sharing something as private as her dreams with anyone. Never, that was, until now.

CHAPTER NINE

"So who is it at the door? Do you know?"

Chloe poked her fork restlessly into bits of lettuce on her plate, pushing aside a cherry tomato and watching as it rolled. She shifted uncomfortably in her seat, not so much at the question but at the stab of pain her answer brought.

"I think it's my mother," she said softly.

Pastor James nodded and took a sip of his iced tea.

"Your mother?"

Chloe looked up without raising her head.

"My real mother."

She reached for the wrapper of her straw and played with it restlessly, winding it around her finger, then unwinding it, then winding it again.

"When's the last time you spoke with your mother?"

"My real mother?" Chloe shrugged and let go a short breath from her nose. "I've never spoken with my real mother. I don't even know who she is. I've never met her."

Bitterness touched at her tone as she spoke, and she slumped against the hard wood backing of the folding chair. The two were seated in the church kitchen, a pitcher of iced tea before them, along with a bowl of day-old salad and fried chicken. Pastor James piled high on his plate a heaping serving of potato salad. Chloe waved away his hand as he attempted to drop a spoonful on her own plate.

He put the plastic container back on the table and regarded her with eyes brimming with compassion.

"I'm sorry."

"Oh, it's fine," Chloe said breezily, picking at her chicken leg and popping a bit of breaded coating in her mouth.

"I mean, plenty of people grow up without their real mothers, right?" She couldn't keep the bitterness out of her voice.

Pastor James, catching her tone, said nothing but tilted his head as if doubtful. Chloe stabbed hard at a cucumber and crunched loudly, then drained her iced tea in one long gulp. She reached for the pitcher but Pastor James grabbed it first and refilled her glass. She watched the golden liquid swirl, chewing distractedly at the inside of her lip as her mind wandered to the past.

"So my mom left me and never bothered to come find me, never bothered to look me up, never bothered to drop me a note in the mail and say—hey, hello there, I'm your mom, just want to let you know," she finally blurted, her voice quiet but her tone hostile.

"So what, right?" It was a sarcastic question, rhetorical in nature. And she jumped when she felt the sudden touch on her hand. Reflexively, she pulled it back. Then she saw his startled face and inwardly cursed her instincts.

"I'm sorry," Pastor James said. "I was just trying to comfort you. I didn't mean to make you jump."

"No, I'm sorry. I know you didn't mean anything. I guess I just—" she faltered for the right words, before finally shrugging in defeat. "I mean, I guess I'm just not used to talking about myself. Or my family. Or anything much, for that matter."

They chewed in silence for a few moments.

"I was just lost in thought," she added. "Just thinking back."

"My dad left my mom and me when I was six," he said suddenly.

Chloe widened her eyes in surprise.

"Are you serious?"

He took a couple bites, wiped his mouth with a paper napkin, and leaned back in his chair. He reached forward with his left hand and rubbed the side of his iced tea glass as he spoke, sliding his thumb and forefinger slowly up and down. Chloe watched the streaks of wetness his fingers left from the condensation of the glass. Almost instinctively, she started counting them. Then she caught herself, stopped, and focused her eyes on his face as he spoke.

"Yep. I still remember the last time I saw him. I was standing at my bedroom window and looking down, watching as he threw his bags in the trunk of his car. It was raining pretty hard and he had on a baseball cap, so I couldn't really see his face. But I was wondering where he was going and I thought maybe he was taking a trip and he was just waiting until the rain stopped to come get me to go with him. I was about to get my coat and shoes and run downstairs to tell him I was ready, and then I saw her."

Chloe sat rapt, waiting for him to continue.

"My mother," he said, his eyes turning a hazy blue as he spoke. "My mother was running over to him—she still had on her robe and slippers, and I thought, well she must be telling him to wait for her to get dressed, she must be telling him to hold on, give her a minute to get ready—I thought that's what was going on."

He paused to clear his throat.

"And then I saw him turn around and step toward her and grab her by the arm and hit her," he said. "He smacked her across the face, and then he smacked her again across the face, and the second time he let go of her arm so when he hit her, she fell on the ground. I think I screamed out then. I think I yelled out, 'Mom!' I don't really remember but I must have, because all of a sudden I saw my dad's face turned up toward me, staring at me through the window, and I could see him, I could see his expression. His mouth was scrunched into this tight little line—that's what I remember the most. It scared me. His face scared me. It looked like pure hate and I knew I should've run down to help my mother, but I was too scared of him. We stared at each other for a second, and then I backed away from the window. I was terrified he saw me looking at him."

He sighed deeply then took a sip from his glass.

"I waited a while. I waited, oh, I don't know how long," he said. "But I waited long enough so I could tell he either wasn't coming upstairs to get me—to hit me for watching him through the window—or that he had gone; that he had gotten in the car and just gone. Then I finally looked out the window again, his car was gone. So was my mother."

"Your mother was gone?"

He looked up and took another sip of tea.

"Yeah. I thought my dad had taken her, but it turned out, she had just gone back in the house." He gave a short humorless laugh. "Thing was, afterward, for the next few hours, I heard these noises in the house and I really thought it was my dad coming to get me. So I hid in my closet all morning. I hid under a pile of dirty clothes in the closet. I must have been there half the day. I didn't come out until I heard my mother's voice calling for me."

He gave another laugh that was more grunt.

"That's when I knew the sounds I heard weren't from my dad, after all. They were hers. I guess she must have been in the kitchen or something, crying," he said. He thought for several moments, and then, almost to the air, said, "I really don't know why she was crying. Maybe it was because he hurt her when he hit her, or maybe it was because he left her all alone." Barely above a whisper, he added, "I hope it wasn't both."

He cleared his throat and took another sip.

"Thing was," he said, sighing deeply and gazing into her face, "I always blamed myself for not saving her after my dad hit her. I always wondered how wet she must have been, lying there on the ground in her robe as the rain poured down. And I always wished that instead of running to hide in my closet I had rushed downstairs and helped her. I could have at least brought her a towel."

"You were six."

"I know." He sounded so dejected when he said it, Chloe reached out and patted his arm. He looked up with a smile, then offered her more salad.

"Take some. The vegetables will help you heal faster."

He watched as Chloe picked up the tongs and sorted through the bowl, placing lettuce, cucumbers and carrots on her plate.

"No tomatoes?"

She made a face.

"Echh."

They ate in silence again for a few moments, then Chloe leaned forward and put down her fork.

"So you never saw him again after that?"

"Nope. Never. To this day, I'm not even sure why he left."

"You didn't ask your mom what happened? Not even when you were an adult?" Chloe couldn't keep the shock from her voice. For a split second, she thought she saw a strange shadow cross his face. Then it was gone and he started speaking again.

"Of course I did. I mean, I did when I was a little kid—I asked her a few times. But her answer was always the same; that things didn't work out and sometimes, that's just how it is in marriage. The couples break up, they grow apart, they move on."

He paused and swallowed hard.

"Honestly, I think she was just embarrassed at how he left. I think she was embarrassed at the memory of him hitting her and leaving her on the ground in the rain, and I don't think she really wanted to remember it at all," he said. "And I didn't really want to push the matter because I didn't think she knew I saw him hitting her, so I just thought it'd be easier to let it all drop. I didn't want to get in a conversation about it where I would either have to lie or tell her the truth of what I saw."

He pushed his fork around his plate, making swirly patterns in the mayonnaise from his potato salad.

"So we didn't talk about any of it," he said. "I never really thought it mattered, though, because it's not like we were just sitting around, waiting for him to come back. We moved on. By the time I was twelve, she was working two jobs, she worked nights and some days, and I had school in the day. We didn't really see each other much, anyway. Then, in the summers, I worked. It was kind of like she did her thing, I did mine. We didn't just not talk about my dad. We didn't talk about much at all."

"Sounds like you kind of raised yourself."

"Well, my mom was always there when I needed her for something. I did theater for a while in eighth grade, and she never missed a play. I tried the chess club in ninth grade and she made it to all my matches—at least most of them. I even went out for basketball in tenth grade and she came to some of my games. Those were at night, so she couldn't easily take off work, but she tried." He stopped, lost in thought. Then he smiled and put down his fork. "But in between her night shifts and my school days, we almost always got together for pancakes and eggs at breakfast. So if there was something I needed, I knew I could always catch her at breakfast."

He took a few hurried bites of his food, then wiped his mouth hard with his napkin and threw it back on the table.

"Anyhow, when I was sixteen, my mom had this dinner planned for us. We were going to go out to a fancy restaurant—she even bought me a suit for my birthday present so I'd have something to wear." He paused and laughed at her puzzled expression. "I know, I know. I know what you're thinking. What kind of birthday present is a suit for a sixteen-year-old guy, right?"

Absently, he lifted a chicken leg and turned it in his hand. Chloe watched with amusement as juice trickled onto his shirt. He wiped futilely with his paper napkin, then grabbed another, then another.

"But thing is, I really liked it. I mean, we weren't rich in the first place. Then, when my dad left, things got really tight. We lost our home, we had to move into this trailer park. We bought clothes at thrift stores and hardly ever went out to eat. We weren't exactly poverty level, but just about. So I know my mom must have planned for a long time to save the money to buy me a suit and then take me out for a really nice dinner."

"Actually," Chloe said, remembering her own sixteenth birthday with sadness, "it does sound pretty nice." She thought back to the party she had snuck out to and the boy who pulled her roughly down the hallway of the host's house and into the bedroom. It's not like that was her first time. But it was the first time she encountered a band of jeering boys who mocked her as she drunkenly made her way back to the main room of the party afterward. It was the first time she encountered cruel whispers and taunts from the lips of his friends, and their girlfriends, in school in the following weeks.

She smiled wistfully at Pastor James's gift of a suit. She would've loved to have had a mom who wanted to dress up and take her out to dinner to celebrate her birthday.

"It was. It was a great surprise," Pastor James said, not noticing Chloe's faraway eyes as his own were fixed somewhere on the wall, staring at his own memories. "And I also thought it might be the perfect time to talk about my dad. I mean, I wasn't going to force the discussion and ruin the evening. But I thought if it seemed like the timing was right, and everything was going well, it might be the perfect opportunity to see about raising the topic." He shrugged, then shrugged again. "I figured it might be the best chance I had to ask her, too, if she knew where he was—where he moved to, where he was living. You know, in case I ever wanted to look him up again."

He took another enormous bite of chicken and once again, wiped furiously with napkins at the juice that dropped on his shirt.

Chloe waited, expecting him to finish the story after he cleaned his mess. But he didn't. He sat there in silence, his eyes glued to his plate, his right hand once again pushing his fork lightly along lumps of potato salad. She searched his face for clues. Finally, she couldn't take it any longer.

"So," she said, "what happened? Did you ask her?"

He raised his face and Chloe saw with shock his eyes had turned watery.

"I never got the chance to," he said quietly. "She ran to the store while I was finishing getting dressed for dinner. She was supposed to be back in just a minute. An hour passed and I was wondering what was taking her so long. Then I got this knock on the door. It was the police. She got hit by a drunk driver. She was pronounced dead at the scene."

Chloe sat in stunned silence. She felt a mix of emotions wash over her, not the least of which was horror at the circumstances of their first meeting.

"I'm sorry," she finally said, biting the tip of her tongue as she tried to think of the right words to explain away her own drinking and driving. She stared hard at her plate, too scared, too ashamed to look him in the eyes, even after he spoke—especially after he spoke.

"I guess you're wondering now why I didn't have you thrown in jail, right?"

Chloe nodded, not daring to lift her head.

"You know, after my mom died, for the longest time, I was angry. I was angry at everyone, I hated everything about my life. I even thought about killing myself." At that, she looked up. "Does that surprise you, a pastor admitting he once wanted to kill himself?"

He cleared his throat and pushed back from the table a few inches.

"Well, it's true. I had to go live with my uncle on his farm in this flyover state where I'd never been, never visited, didn't know anyone. And the town where my uncle lived had something like 100 residents. The school I went to had a class size of thirty. To call it the boonies was being generous."

Chloe smiled, trying to picture the spiky hair in the middle of farm country, trying to imagine how he got along at school.

"There wasn't much to do there—besides work on the farm, which I didn't much care for. And there weren't many kids my age to hang around with—besides this one guy who lived up the road who was always stuck in the house with some sort of sickness. I think he got worn down easy, always had to rest. I never really got the full story on him, but it was something about his thyroid. Anyway, so I fell in with a couple of guys from the next town over who were old enough to buy beer and alcohol and they had their own truck. That was my life; hanging with them, getting drunk, stealing stuff, riding around and smashing mailboxes, and picking up girls. That was how I spent the next couple years."

Chloe's mouth fell open, but she said nothing.

"My uncle got tired of the cops bringing me home, so he told me that once I turned eighteen, I had to go. I told him I'd leave now if he wanted. Of course, I cussed him out a bit as I was saying it." Pastor James shook his head at the memory. "I was such an idiot."

"Did you leave?"

"Yep. I cut out that night. Just grabbed my bag, flipped off my uncle, and headed to my buddy's home. I figured he'd either leave with me or at least give me a ride to the bus station so I could take off by myself. I forgot how long a walk it was, though, and my shoulders were getting tired from hauling my stuff. It must have been around mid-night—I still had a ways to go—so I decided I'd just lay down and take a quick nap by the side of the road. Found myself a tree—more like a bush, really—a bit up the way and threw my stuff down, stretched out, and started to shut my eyes."

He stopped talking and stared intently at his fingers, lightly rubbing his right thumb along the nails on his left hand.

"I started to shake a little," he said hesitantly. He paused and stared at his nails. "And not from the cold or from fear or anything like that. I started to shake a little because I was dying for something to drink. I started sweating and I felt nauseous and anxious and weak and I was shaking, like I said. I got really angry because I knew I didn't have anything to drink, and I also knew I still had a long way to go before I got to my friend's home, and it wasn't likely a car was going to drive by that I could hitch for a ride. I mean, I was stuck in the middle of nowhere, in the middle of the country at midnight, nobody around—who was going to happen by?"

He raised his hands, palms open, and smiled.

"But like I said, I was dying for a drink—some beer, some alcohol, heck, I think I'd have sucked down cough syrup if I had any with me. But I had nothing. And I got so angry I just started yelling." He laughed at the memory. "Yep, right there, right in the dark, I just started cursing like a sailor, screaming at my mom, ticked off my mom died, screaming at my dad, ticked off my dad left, yelling at my uncle, screaming about living with lousy hicks, screaming out how much I hated God, how I didn't believe in Him, cursing Him with the vilest curses I could think of. And you know what happened?"

Chloe sat, wide-eyed, waiting.

"This star streaked across the sky and then this amazing light seemed to explode at the end of the streak, and it was like something whispered in my ear—only it wasn't in my ear, it was more like in my heart, in my soul—but it was a voice I felt more than heard, and it said, 'God loves you.'"

Chloe gulped hard, fighting the sudden hard ball that formed in her throat.

"Are you serious?"

"And then I felt this wave of warm come over me, and I felt completely at peace. I can't explain it. Even today," he said, shaking his head vigorously, "I can't fully explain it. All I know is I saw the star, saw the light, felt this incredible peaceful feeling, and all my anger went away."

She watched as he sipped his tea, taking in all he had said. Questions bubbled in her mind, but she wasn't sure which to ask, if any.

"So," Pastor James said, pushing his arms straight into the side of the table and stretching as far back as he could lean, "after that, I just didn't feel angry anymore. I started looking around and seeing how stupid it was for me to be in the middle of nowhere, with no plan in life. I ended up going back to my uncle's house and we worked things out." He stopped and gave her a somber look, then sat forward, so his face was just inches from hers. "It wasn't easy. I had to go to rehab for my drinking. But I can tell you I've never touched a drop of alcohol since that time—and I've never even wanted to, if you want to know the truth."

"So how did you get to be a pastor?"

Pastor James chuckled.

"Oh, did I forget to mention, my uncle was also a pastor? He was a farmer full-time, but every Sunday, he led the con-gregation at the little country church forty miles from his farm. I started going to church with him when I got out of rehab"—Pastor James let out a long and loud laugh—"and I never did stop."

He started putting the covers back on the food dishes and stacking his silverware on his plate. Chloe sat and watched, digesting all he told her and debating whether to say something was tugging at her heart.

"You know," she finally said, watching him carefully as she spoke, "the last thing from my wreck I remember seeing, before I woke up at the hospital, anyway, was the sticker on your car that said, 'God loves you.' Then I saw it again a couple more times since." She felt her face redden and she looked away.

"He does love you," Pastor James said simply. "Just like He loves me. And what's more," he said, standing and balancing Chloe's plate and silverware on top of his, "it's no accident you're here."

He took her plate and scraped off the remains of her food into the trash, then placed it alongside his in the sink. She watched as he rinsed the dishes, added some soap, then scrubbed them with a sponge and laid them on a towel on the counter to dry.

"So if you're wondering why I'm not angry that you were drinking the night you hit me, and if you're wondering why I don't want you in jail, and if you're wondering why I am helping you get back on your feet," he said, turning toward her and leaning his back against the sink, "this is why: There but for the grace of God go I." He paused, letting the words sink in, and then adding, "It's a famous saying based on the Bible."

Chloe nodded, not fully understanding, but understanding enough. He watched her in silence for a moment. Then once again, Chloe was shocked by what he said.

"We just lost our math teacher at our Christian school. She quit. Suddenly—just like that," he said, snapping his fingers. "How would you like to be our new math teacher? I know you don't have a teaching degree but we could help you get a certificate, if you want. You could keep doing the record-keeping and financials of the church for the free room and board, but then you could collect the math teacher salary as well. And you could do it just temporarily, if you like, until we find a full-time replacement—but who knows, maybe you'll like it enough to want to stay on as the permanent teacher." She gasped out loud. "Really?"

"For real?"

Behind him, above the sink, hung a picture with a silver frame with black lettering on three of its four sides: One side read "God." The second side read "Loves." And the third read "You."

Chloe sighed as she read it, then with a small smile and shake of her head, stopped fighting it.

"Sounds great," she said. "It really sounds great."

For the first time in a long time, she slept the entire night without waking.

CHAPTER TEN

"It's not that hard really," she said, reaching for the ledger and flipping to the income and expense sheet. "You had a discrepancy of forty-five cents here—" and she pointed to a line, glancing at James before continuing, "and that's why this wouldn't balance."

After all these months, he still couldn't properly total his expenses. Chloe stole a look at his baffled face and burst out laughing.

"You look like a llama," she said.

"What?"

He had a way of scrunching his face when confused that reminded her of a llama she once saw in a petting zoo as a little girl. She had held out a hand filled with pellets, expecting it to come running, but the llama instead gazed at her wide-eyed and blankly, its head tilted far to the side as if mulling a deep philosophical matter.

"I don't know," she said, turning back to the books. "You just do."

She tapped with authority at the pages in front of her.

"Look," she said. "Errors that are divisible by nine are usually due to someone writing down a number in the wrong order. Like seventy-two, when they mean twenty-seven. So I just looked for that—and here—" she broke off, engrossed in her tabulations. "I could've sworn I told you this before," she said, almost to herself. After a few moments, she slapped triumphantly again at the page.

"Here it is. You can see that's exactly what happened."

Chloe's voice drifted off as she slowly turned pages, her eyes flowing past figures, her mind quickly adding here, subtracting there. She paused, looking into the distance, frowning, then back to Pastor James's face. She started to speak, but then abruptly changed her mind and slapped shut the book.

Her eyes clouded at a disturbing thought she was turning in her mind. She had grown quite fond of James the past few months they worked together, and she was hoping she was wrong. It wouldn't be an easy conversation, she knew, if she were right.

"I don't know how you do it," he said, straightening his back and feeling with his fingers as his neck muscles popped. "If math is the law of the universe, you certainly are a keeper of that key."

She didn't return his smile, and for a second he wondered at the dark expression in her eyes. Then he smiled broadly and patted her arm reassuringly.

"Don't worry," he said, misinterpreting her serious expression, "You have job security, no matter what kind of budget the church has going forward."

He shuffled papers from his desk to put them into his backpack. Chloe watched with furrowed brows. For weeks, she had been trying to get him to organize his church documents in clearly marked file folders, and to carry them in something better than a backpack. She even bought him a briefcase at a second-hand store and shined it so the leather glowed. But he refused to use it, mocking it as white-collar wear.

"How would it look if I visited homeless at the shelter looking like a million bucks?" he'd asked, after thanking her, nonetheless, for the gift and running his fingertips softly over the brown case. "I'll save this for when I go to church conferences."

He scrunched the papers into a roll, making Chloe wince, then shoved them deeper and zipped it closed. Tossing it to the floor, he plopped in his seat and turned to her.

"I've heard lots of good feedback from your students about your teaching."

Chloe's eyes brightened. She loved teaching math. More than that, she loved seeing the kids' faces light up when they finally grasped something she was teaching. It never got old; she would float for hours after class, playing and replaying in her mind the moment when a struggling student suddenly understood. The lightbulb was palpable and every time it clicked on—every time she helped click it on—Chloe felt a surge of joy.

She had never felt such purpose in life.

"They say you have a way of making math seem important—you make it seem like math is something that actually matters, and it's not just about doing classwork." He stood and reached for his bag, threw it over his shoulders and gave her a quick pat on the shoulder. "The other teachers like you too. Mrs. Hagerty, especially. She says her son hasn't ever been able to subtract and divide that well, and percentages were a mystery to him, but now, in just a few short weeks, he's solving problems in his head. He doesn't even need scrap paper half the time."

Chloe's chest burned at the praise and she smiled widely. But she dropped her eyes and refused to meet his gaze. She didn't want him guessing something was bothering her,

155

especially since she was yet to confirm any bother was warranted.

"That's great to hear," she said. "I really like teaching here too."

She loved it, in fact, so much she couldn't stop casting worried eyes at the ledger in her lap as she spoke. She dreaded her suspicions might prove true and somehow jeopardize the happy life she had carved out the last seven months. Bitterness and fear gripped her heart at the thought of losing all—really, of losing any. She glanced at James, imagining his reaction if the worst proved true.

It wouldn't be pleasant, she thought mournfully.

"Well," he said, his blue eyes piercing her as she avoided his look once again, "I guess I'll let you get back to your work then."

Chloe strained hard to smile.

"Thank you." She watched him turn the door handle. Then something made her shout his name.

"Pastor James!" Her voice sounded desperate even in her own ears, and she hastily laughed as he turned, trying to soften her sharpness.

"I just want to say thank you for everything. I mean, the job, the room, the church." Her eyes glistened as she searched his face. "Really, I want to thank you for giving me a chance."

"Of course," he said, giving her an odd look. "You're very welcome." He stood for a moment, as if considering whether or not to leave. Then he smiled.

"God loves you," he said, pulling the door behind him.

As soon as she heard the click, Chloe moved into action.

She yanked open desk drawers and sifted through file after file, pulling out stacks of folders and then pouring over the papers inside the folders and files. After a few minutes, she set aside one manila folder, then another, and put the rest back in the drawers. Grabbing a blank legal pad, a red pen and a pencil, opening the ledger, and laying it on her lap, she went to work.

Two hours later, her fears realized, she sat staring at the wall, wondering how exactly to tell Pastor James his church had been robbed of $48,000 over the past year and a half. Making matters worse, the only person who could have done it was his best friend.

Chloe jumped at the sudden rapping and turned just in time to see Pastor James peek his head through the cracked door.

"Dinner?"

Chloe glanced to the clock.

Normally, his habit of grabbing her for dinner was welcome. They would unwind over coffee and church cafeteria food in the lounge area, or the kitchen, or on a couple of occasions, in the meeting hall by the fireplace. The food wasn't great, but the conversations were always meaningful and interesting. They often traded areas of expertise—he would talk about God and the Gospels and help her understand his Sunday morning messages so she could her solidify her growing faith and she would tell him the mysteries of math: why equations, for instance, can be used to determine the shortest routes for mail delivery and how on occasion, while waitressing, she would compute how many flips of the spatula it would take to put a stack of pancakes in order by size, smallest down to largest.

"Isn't that funny," he said about the pancakes. "Catholics often eat pancakes on Shrove Tuesday, the final feast day before their forty days of Lent." They had shared a good laugh on that.

"Pancakes—who knew? Mathematical and religious," Chloe had replied.

Somberly, Chloe looked at the papers before her, covered in red scribbles and pencil slashes. *There won't be much laughter at tonight's dinner*, she thought.

But she had to go. She had to have the discussion.

"Sure," she told him, with as breezy a manner she could manage. She clapped shut the ledger and scooped her papers together.

"Do you mind if I show you something, though?" She pulled the ledger tight to her chest and scooted out the door in front of him, avoiding his curious glance. "Where should we eat tonight?"

He paused, watching her face closely, then shrugged.

"Cafeteria's good for me."

They walked in stilted silence and Chloe didn't bother to wait for him to hold the door for her when they arrived. She pushed it open absently and headed right for a table. She flopped into the closest seat and with a sigh, carefully laid the ledger and papers on the table. She kept her hand on top, as if protecting the pages beneath or perhaps, shielding their secrets from other eyes. Her eyes were fixed on the stack. Over and over, she counted the letters of the ledger: *L, one; E, two; D, three*; and so forth, several times, until he, too, sat and broke the silence.

"Okay. Let's get to what's been bothering you before we eat."

He fixed her with a steady, clear gaze, and Chloe shuffled her papers uncomfortably, wishing she could be anywhere but in front of those eyes. She didn't want to watch as they turned dark.

Her mind flashed to her beginning days at the church, to the time she overheard his disagreement with the office woman, Tammy, and for several moments, she fought the impulse to flee, to hurl the papers onto the floor and just run from the church. She had not been in the room during his discussion with Tammy, but she caught his tone, heard the rising tension in his words, and from the safety of her borrowed bed, she pictured his face—the change in his eyes from calm to stormy. It was the same change that used to come over her father when he was roused to anger; a flip of the switch and like that, his demeanor would change.

She watched James now with wariness. She wasn't afraid of his anger; rather, she was deeply saddened at the idea of bringing pain to his life, and watching it unfold in his eyes and face.

"Hey. What's wrong?"

Chloe cleared her throat.

"I found some missing money from your church," she blurted, and from there, the words tumbled. "I was going through the accounts and found a bunch of checks from a few months ago that were out of sequence, all made out to the same organization, all signed by the same person, all for the same amounts. Four checks, all for $12,000 each."

She watched his face for reaction. His eyes turned a slightly darker hue, and she glanced at the stack of papers for a moment before continuing.

"But when I looked at where the money was taken from, I saw it all came from the savings that was supposed to be used for church school expenses. The checks were drawn from the facilities account—the one for expanding the school building."

She sifted through the papers until she found the copies she had made of the checks and slid then slightly toward him. Her hands shook a little, but he refused to touch them. He simply glanced at them, then back at her.

"Who wrote them?"

Chloe gulped and tapped at the papers set before him, hoping he'd save her from having to speak the rest out loud.

"No," he said, sitting back in his chair and crossing his arms. "You tell me. Who wrote them?"

"Robert Ducetti," she said quietly.

She jumped in surprise as he shot his chair back hard, scraping the legs loudly against the floor.

"What!"

His mouth was wide with shock and he stared with such intensity, Chloe sat completely still, paralyzed by his eyes. They glared black, looking not so much at Chloe as through her. She let out her breath slowly, waiting for him to speak.

When he did, his voice was so calm it alarmed her even more.

"My best friend did not steal from me." He folded his arms on his chest and pursed his lips tight.

"I suggest you check the books again."

Chloe bit her lip and wished she could just agree with him, then escape and pretend to check again—and then maybe even let the whole matter drop, or even lie, and say she was wrong. But something within her wouldn't let her take the easy way out. She just couldn't lie to him and pretend everything was fine.

"I've checked a dozen times," she whispered.

The seconds of silence that followed were agonizing.

But she kept her eyes fixed on his, hoping he might read the truth in them and then she could be his sympathetic ear while he figured out the best way to deal with the situation. What came next was far from her imaginations, though.

He leaned his hands on the table, spreading his fingers wide and tilting his head close. In a tight voice, eyes unblinking, he half spoke, half hissed.

"There wasn't any missing money until you came."

Her mouth dropped in shock.

"Don't you think that's an interesting coincidence?"

For a moment, Chloe considered he might be kidding; that he might be playing a cruel joke as a way of deflecting from his anger about his friend. But then she realized he was serious. As she gazed into his dark eyes, she felt the fury rise in her own body.

"Screw you!"

She only wished she hadn't shouted it—that she instead matched his even-level tone with her own even-level response. Then she saw his eyes widen in shock, and she felt better.

"Screw you and screw this," she said, sweeping her arms wildly at the ledger on the table, sending papers flying to the floor and the book crashing against a wall.

She stormed from the room and down the hallway to her room, grabbing her jacket and stuffing some of her belongings into a plastic bag she fished from the trash can. Her eye fell on the leather backpack James had given her as a congratulations gift the day her cast was removed, but scornfully, she kicked it aside and shoved clothes she wrenched from the closet into another plastic bag that lay on her bureau, filled with the items she just purchased at the convenience store. Finally, she threw in her toothbrush and toothpaste, slammed the bathroom door as loud as she could, and then slammed the bedroom door even louder.

Breathing hard, she strode to the church exit and just before pulling on the door handle, turned her head and shouted one more time. It was childish, she knew; but she didn't care. She counted the faces of shocked church staffers who quickly peeked from their offices, then just as quickly pulled back inside: *one, two, three, four.* She felt smug satisfaction at their dismay and hoped they would tell the pastor.

She pulled hard on the door and for a second, stood stunned. An open-mouthed man in a gray suit was grabbing the arm of the woman in a bright yellow dress and pulling her tightly to him. Chloe paused, waiting for them to step aside. She glared as she walked past and didn't look back as she felt their stares. Still angry, she reached the edge of the parking lot, where it met the road, and without turning her head, lifted a long arm into the air and extended her middle finger.

She had no idea if Pastor James saw. But as the tears welled and she cursed her weakness and wiped at her cheeks, she prayed he did. Then her plastic bag ripped, spilling the contents of her dresser and drawers onto the roadway. Chloe kicked at a shampoo bottle, then a container of deodorant, and stubbornly left the rest on the ground.

By the time Pastor James made it to the doorway, all he saw was a small scattered selection of multi-colored objects at the bend in the road and a woman in a yellow dress with a young man in a perfectly pressed suit standing awkwardly to the side of the church foyer.

CHAPTER ELEVEN

"Well, look what the cat dragged in."

Chloe looked at the woman standing before her and spread her arms wide, palms up, fingers slightly curled.

"What can I say. It's been a while," Chloe said, smiling.

Marjorie sniffed. Reaching down, she scratched her left shin loudly, sending a flurry of white flakes onto the ground as she did. Chloe pretended not to see and bit the urge to wave her hands at the air.

"So," Marjorie said, drawing deeply on a cigarette she pulled from her pocket and lit. "Whatcha want?"

Chloe sighed and tried to sound nonchalant, watching the trail of Marjorie's smoke as it floated across the doorstep. She stiffened, fighting the impulse to step back, and turned her head slightly as she answered so she wouldn't breathe in smoke. She noticed Marjorie watching her, so she pretended she was looking at a bird in the nearby yard.

"Well, my job back, for one. You know if Tony's hiring?"

Marjorie snorted and laughed.

"Tony's always hiring." She looked Chloe up and down slowly. "But I dunno if he's hiring you. You did kind of leave him in a bind, you know. Just walking off and all, no notice, nothing."

Chloe nodded but said nothing. She glanced sidewise at the rip in the thigh on Marjorie's jeans, so high up the pink lace of her underwear peeked through. She pulled her eyes away, before Marjorie noticed. But then she caught a glimpse of Marjorie's bra strap sticking out from her shoulder, a dingy yellow with hanging threads, and that led her eyes to drift to the large circular stain right in the middle of her too-tight white t-shirt. The stain, Chloe saw, with near fascination, was almost the exact same color as Marjorie's bra strap.

Marjorie cleared her throat and with a start, Chloe looked up, wondering how long she had been staring. By the look in Marjorie's eyes, she figured long enough to cause offense.

"So," Chloe said, smiling widely, "how have things been with you?"

Marjorie, obviously insulted, jutted out her chin and took another deep pull of her cigarette, blowing it purposely at Chloe's face.

"What do you care? I haven't heard from you in a year. Now all of a sudden you show up on my doorstep and want to be friends?"

Chloe shuffled her feet at her hostile tone and stood silent.

"What? Nothing to say? You got nothing at all to say?"

The silence stretched uncomfortably long and Chloe, already worn from the ordeal at the church, was about to turn in defeat and leave, when Marjorie spoke again.

"How'd you get here, anyway?" Her voice was friendlier, and Chloe flashed another smile.

"I got a ride with a guy," she said, truthfully. A passing trucker took pity on her walk in the middle of nowhere and, curious about her plastic bag of clothing, stopped and offered a ride. Chloe hesitated, not liking the way he leered, but then she remembered the pastor's accusation. She jumped right in the cab.

"He dropped me off about a mile from here," she said, leaving unstated it was actually she who demanded he pull over and let her out, after his hands wouldn't quit wandering from the wheel and into her lap. The mile-long walk gave her plenty of time to curse out the pastor for putting her in the position of having to deal with the truck driver. Any doubts she had about going to Marjorie's disappeared during that hike. "You want a beer or something?" Her tone, while not exactly soft, had lost its angry edge and Chloe gave a half-hearted but grateful smile.

"Why not," she said, slowly climbing the steps, glad at the chance to sit. Marjorie held the door open wide with one arm, blowing smoke hard directly into Chloe's face as she passed. Chloe groaned and made a face, making Marjorie laugh.

"Yeah, that's right. I did that on purpose." She laughed again and let the door slam shut. "It's the least you deserve for blowing me off so freaking long." Marjorie flashed her two middle fingers and chuckled at Chloe's wide eyes.

"It's okay," she said, clapping Chloe on the shoulder. "All's forgiven now."

Chloe jerked a bit at Marjorie's crudeness.

A stab of sadness hit at her as she looked at the beer cans and whiskey bottles strewn alongside a pile of dirty underwear on the corner of the ripped couch and thought of the clean white comforter and fluffy pillows that were her nighttime refuge for the last few months. She sniffed, wrinkling her nose at the stale smells of lingering tobacco smoke and what appeared to be some sort of dried spaghetti sauce on a plastic plate on top of the trash barrel. Briefly, Chloe wondered why it wasn't inside the trashcan, but then saw, as she walked slowly by, it was because there was no room. The bag was busting with trash, and she swatted roughly the tiny little gnats encircling her face. Quickly, she stepped into the living room, watching as Marjorie pushed clothes and overflowing ashtrays to the side to make room on the couch for Chloe to sit.

"What the—" Chloe jumped to her feet, feeling her backside with one nervous hand while looking anxiously at the cushion. "Why'm I wet?"

Marjorie burst out in a raucous laugh that ended in coughs. She stamped out her cigarette butt, then almost at the same time, reached for another.

"I dunno. I forgot I put my wet laundry there earlier. The dryer doesn't work, ya know," she said, giving Chloe a look that was almost accusing. "Not everybody has a dryer," she added.

Chloe said nothing, but moved a few inches to her left and cautiously took a seat.

"Gum?" Marjorie ripped open the wrapper of a stick after Chloe refused and tossed it into her mouth. Chewing loudly, she rolled the wrapper between her thumb and forefinger into a tight little ball, then hurled it into the corner of the room. It landed on top of her laundry pile. She felt around the cushion and pulled forth her box of cigarettes. She lit the one she was holding then offered the box to Chloe.

"Uh, thanks. No, thanks, though."

Marjorie regarded her with surprise.

"What, you quit?" She said it in the tone of disbelief. Then she shrugged and stretched lazily on the couch. "Oh well, more for me then. You always did bum half my cigarettes from me, anyway."

Chloe began to wonder about her students and who'd they get to replace her as math teacher. She gulped hard, fighting back sudden tears. *This is my future now*, she thought dismally, staring at a stain of food on the wall right next to the garbage can. *This is where I belong.* The thought sunk deep and within a few moments, she felt the pity disappear and a slow boil anger take its place. Then rebellion set and she turned to Marjorie with a scowl.

"Here, gimme one of those," she said, holding out her hand and taking both cigarette and lighter. Quickly, before she could give herself time to change her mind, she flicked the lighter and sucked deep. Dark smoke filled her lungs, and in agony, she fought to expel it. For several moments, she coughed and choked, and coughed some more, until her eyes filled with water. Marjorie's mocking laughter rang in the background, and Chloe turned her head in embarrassment.

"You did quit. You idiot." Marjorie stood and walked to the fridge, removed a can and shoved it into Chloe's hand. "Here, drink this."

Chloe glanced at the beer and paused, a Bible passage the pastor once shared popping into her mind, something about being a child and walking as a child, but then putting the childhood ways behind.

She forced the thought away and clicked open the can. *Screw him*, she thought again, but with a touch of sadness. Quickly, she drank.

It had been months since she tasted beer, and for a second or two, Chloe feared it was going to go the way of the cigarette. Then she swallowed hard and took another deep gulp. By the third, she felt in control enough to flash a smile at Marjorie and lean comfortably into the cushion.

A wave of warmth rushed through her body, and Chloe cooled it by taking more sips. Before she knew it, the can was empty. Triumphant, she crushed it on the coffee table and giggled when Marjorie slapped her on the back.

"Guess you haven't forgotten how to drink, at least," Marjorie said, cracking open her own beer. "For a minute there, you had me worried."

"You can take the girl out the party, but you can't take the party of the girl, right?" Chloe's head was already beginning to buzz. "How about another?"

Marjorie pointed at the fridge.

"It's self-serve," she said. "I'm not your freaking waitress."

"Some things never change," Chloe said, her head in the fridge. "A fridge full of beer, with just a pack of crackers and a piece of toast for food." Chloe grabbed a six-pack and brought it to the table with the crackers. "Johnny still around too?"

"Johnny?" Marjorie spit out a string of adjectives, stamping her cigarette violently on a nearby plate. "I threw him out a month ago. You know what he did? Hooked up with that white trash Paula, that's what he did. Freaking cheater. Cheaters always cheat."

"Yes they do," Chloe said, in a sing-songy voice as she sunk back on the couch.

Marjorie sucked hard at the beer flowing from the top of the can, catching as much as she could before it dripped on to her lap. Chloe popped open another can, took a deep swig, then reached again for the cigarette pack. Marjorie grabbed it and held it high above her head, as if keeping it away from a toddler. Finally, she relented and pulled one from the pack.

"Fine. Here," Marjorie said, tossing a cigarette at Chloe's lap. "But if you waste this one, no more."

Chloe lit it and struggled to keep from coughing. She blew hard then quickly sipped beer, hoping to put out the burn in her lungs before it choked her. She spent the next few minutes lightly inhaling, then following each exhale with a few sips of beer. After she got the hang, she began to suck in smoke as deeply as Marjorie.

"Hey, I know," Marjorie said, reaching for the coffee table, but misjudging the distance and bouncing to the floor. Undeterred, she pulled at the remote control and flipped on the television. "It's almost time for my game show."

The booming sound of a man's voice filled the room, and Chloe nearly dropped her can.

"Geesh, Marj, turn it down!"

"I am, I am, I am, am I," she mumbled, mixing up her words as she drunkenly fiddled with the remote.

"God loves you!" boomed the voice on the TV set. Chloe stared at the screen, but just then, his face disappeared and a big wheel with numbers took his place.

"Holy crap," Marjorie said, laughing as she let the remote fall back on the table. "Got that crap off there fast." She pulled herself with difficulty back to her chair. "I didn't even know they had these stupid church shows this late at night. I thought that was a Sunday morning thing."

Chloe said nothing. But she could've sworn, in the brief seconds the man's face was on the screen, he was the same pastor on the television show at the hospital.

"Here, finish this for me," Marjorie said, handing her an opened can. She reached for another one behind her pillow and cracked the top. "I got another one right here."

Chloe turned from the television and with a shrug, sucked deeply until the can was empty. Then she took the last few from the fridge and put them on the coffee table.

"So we don't have to move during the show," she said, pointing to the cans and hiccupping heavily.

"Great idea," Marjorie said, stretching on the floor and shutting her eyes. For the next half hour, Chloe drank as Marjorie slept. She woke with a start when the audience cheered and credits ran across the screen.

"What'd I miss," she said, sitting up groggily and wiping her eyes.

"You missed that the beer's all gone." She lifted her finger and waved about a plastic strap and shook lightly the dangling empty cans. She hadn't even bothered to take them out of their plastic ring before drinking them. Chloe burst out laughing and threw the cans toward the trash, missing the mark by several feet.

"Oh nooooooo," Marjorie moaned, her hands striking her head in mock panic. "We'll have to get more," she announced, holding out her hands for Chloe to help her stand. "What time is it?" she asked, looking around wildly.

Chloe pointed to the microwave. "Two fifteen," she said, peering at the green lit numbers.

"Two fifteen! This sucks, Chloe. This sucks. I gotta be at work in a few hours." Marjorie mumbled something incomprehensible, then fell back onto her chair.

Chloe lay flat on her back on the floor and stared at the ceiling, counting tiles, counting food splotches.

"Well, I got to find a work to be at in a few hours," Chloe said.

Marjorie burst out laughing, as if that were the funniest thing she ever heard and went to slap Chloe on the foot, but missed and hit her own shoe instead.

"So," she said, after several seconds passed in silence. "Where were you, anyway? Where'd ya go?" Marjorie burped loudly and swallowed as she burped again.

Chloe sighed and reached for another cigarette. She was getting used to the taste of them.

"Well, I had a wreck. I was in a bad wreck."

Marjorie struggled to sit up, then thought better of it and flopped back onto the hard floor.

"You was in a wreck? What happened? Did someone get hurt?"

"Yeah, I did. I broke my leg and then I had all these cuts and bruises. I couldn't walk for the longest time. I was in the hospital forever."

"Were you in a coma?" Marjorie sat up, this time successfully, and stared hard at Chloe, before drifting her eyes to somewhere in the distance. "You know, my brother was in coma before. He got in a swimming accident. He fell out of a boat or somefin like that. I forget 'zactly what." She hiccupped, and her head sunk to her chest for a moment. Then she bobbed it back up, as if remembering. "Oh, I know what it was. He got hit on the back of the head when he fell on the cooler they had on the boat. He slipped and fell and hit his head on the cooler." She thought hard a moment and turned to check one of the beer cans within reach. She grabbed it and watched as it promptly slipped through her fingers to the floor. Chloe watched as the carpet near her head turned a deeper shade of mustard yellow.

"Yeah, that was it," Marjorie said absently.

"He gotta coma from the coola," she mumbled, repeating it until it almost turned into a jingle. They fell asleep that way, Chloe on her back on the floor and Marjorie, slurring out the last lyrical words until her head was too heavy to hold and she let it drop to her shoulder. She woke two hours later with such a crick, she couldn't turn her neck, and in a panic, still groggy from drink, started kicking her legs to stand. Unfortunately for Chloe, she didn't watch where she kicked.

"Ow!" Chloe grabbed her head in pain. "Son of a—!"

"Sorry!" Marjorie slipped off her chair and onto the floor next to Chloe, rubbing the side of her neck and groaning. "Oh man, this is killing." She peered out the window, squinting at the streetlight that shone brightly. "What time is it anyway?"

Chloe didn't bother to answer; she rolled onto her stomach and lay with her cheek against the dirty carpet, trying to keep from vomiting. The room was spinning and she moaned loudly.

"Why did I drink?" she said. "Why?" She rolled her tongue in her mouth, tasting the dry, stale aftermath of beer and cigarettes. She smacked her lips in disgust and pushed herself slowly to her knees. The room slowed its spinning and she took deep breaths until the nausea passed. Still, the taste lingered on her tongue and she licked her lips uncomfortably, feeling little bits of balled gooey sourness. She reached up and picked them off with her fingers, wiping her hands on her thighs in disgust.

"Come on, Chloe. I gotta get to work. And if you want to see about getting your job back, you gotta get ready too."

Chloe groaned again. The room may have stopped spinning, but her head felt thick and heavy. She thought of the bathtub in her room and the church, and the bubbles that overflowed when she filled it to the top with hot water. She doubted Marjorie's bathroom would be so welcoming—or clean.

"You can shower first," Marjorie said, pulling herself with great difficulty to her feet. "I'm gonna make some coffee." Marjorie lit a cigarette, then held it out for Chloe to take. Groaning again, Chloe shook her head. The smell of fresh smoke was making the taste of stale tobacco in her mouth even stronger, and Chloe turned away quickly, fighting the urge to gag.

"Oh, and you've got clothes in my closet," Marjorie said. "They're in a box in the back. I had some you let me borrow before, and I forgot to return." At that, Chloe smiled sarcastically. Marjorie was famous for her borrowing that turned into keeping.

"But your landlord let me grab some of your clothes too," she added. At that, Chloe looked confused and Marjorie explained, "I went to your home to find out what happened to you and your landlord said he was kicking you out, and clearing out all your stuff. I talked him into letting me get some of your clothes." She paused to take several deep drags of her cigarette. "What a jerk he was about it, though. I practically had to beg him to let me."

Chloe didn't know what to say, but Marjorie sat there staring at her for so long, she felt compelled to say something.

"Oh, thanks," she finally said. "Thanks a lot."

Satisfied, Marjorie smiled and went to make coffee, and Chloe stumbled into the bedroom and slid open the cheap plastic folding door on the closet. It was stuffed and Chloe worked to separate the tangled hangers from each other so she could push them to the side and see her box. Finally, she just pulled out a whole section of clothing and dumped it on the bed. She was starting to sweat.

In the space she had cleared, she saw a brown cardboard box with bright pink and black material peeking from the top.

"Finally," she muttered, tugging at the corners of the cardboard and sliding the box into the light of the bedroom. The pink and black were part of a favorite dress she wore during her bar hopping days.

She held it up and chuckled. It barely fell to mid-thigh. On impulse, she pulled off her shirt and pants and slipped on the dress. Smoothing the tight knit over her torso and adjusting the hem so it hung straight, she stepped to Marjorie's full-length mirror behind the door.

The girl staring back was strangely unrecognizable.

Her hair was in disarray and her eyes sunken, deepened even more by dark, purplish pits that stretched on either side of her nose. Her lips were a strange yellowish hue, and her skin, equally sallow. She tried to smile but quickly clamped her mouth closed. Her unbrushed teeth were the color of milky coffee. She put an open hand to her mouth, blew into her palm and quickly turned her face at the odor.

But it was the dress that really shocked.

Even pulled to its farthest point, the hem barely covered Chloe's bottom. She twisted and turned in the mirror, remembering how she used to wear the dress with thigh-high boots in the winter, and stiletto heels in the summer. It fit her perfectly.

It didn't fit her at all.

Embarrassed at the memories the dress brought, she tore it off her body and rolled it as tight as it could roll, then stuffed the ball of cloth into the bottom of the box. She found a pair of jeans and sweatshirt in the box and headed to the bathroom.

The warm water felt good on her face and she shut her eyes, letting the soap slide off her body, taking with it the tensions of the last day. Her mind drifted to Pastor James, and idly, she wondered what he would think about her pink and black dress. The thought jolted her eyes open and she gasped. Then she thought of her drinking and smoking, and the way they had parted ways, and his face during their last supper together, and she cursed out loud. But it was hard to fool herself. Chloe didn't want to admit that if she could think of an easy way to smooth things over, or to even go back in time and erase what happened, she would happily go back to the church. She already missed her students, her job. More than that—and this is the part she really hated admitting—she missed James too.

It was easier to stay angry than deal with regret and sadness.

"Screw him!" she hissed, rinsing shampoo from her hair then stepping onto the bathmat and rubbing herself dry with a washcloth, the only clean towel Chloe could find.

"Hey, don't use all the hot water." Marjorie banged on the bathroom door, snapping Chloe out of her reverie. "I need to take a shower too."

Chloe dressed and opened the door, her wet hair leaving dark circles on the back of her sweatshirt.

"Did you use all the hot water?"

"No, I don't think so." She took the washcloth and rubbed the ends of her hair again, then stepped aside to let Marjorie into the bathroom. "So," she said, hesitantly, watching as Marjorie squatted and turned on the hot water faucet in the shower and held her hand beneath the flow. "So, do you think I can stay with you for a few days? Umm, maybe for a little longer? Until I get enough money to get a place on my own?"

Marjorie looked up and shrugged.

"I knew you were going to ask me that." She ran her fingers back and forth beneath the water, before finally shutting the faucet and standing. "Well, I guess so. I mean, you did leave me some hot water, so it's fine."

Chloe smiled and gave a thumbs-up.

CHLOE

"Any coffee left?" Chloe stepped to the bedroom door, then called back, almost as a second thought, "I'm gonna take one of your cigarettes, Okay? I'll meet you outside."

She shut the door before Marjorie could argue and glanced at the clock in the kitchen. Pastor James would be sticking his head in her office about this time, for the usual morning prayer session. She smirked as she lit her cigarette. Praying was so stupid, she decided.

Her head was turned to blow the smoke away from the direction of the wind, so she didn't see the small van rolling by with its sticker on the rear bumper that read, "God loves you." But at the same time the van passed, Chloe felt an overwhelming urge to throw up—so strong, she actually bent at the waist and crouched low to the ground, preparing for the worst.

"Oh, God!" she cried in distress, as wave after wave of nausea hit her. She threw her cigarette into the street and braced herself with both hands against the cement steps of Marjorie's home, hoping at the least nobody was watching. Seconds passed, then minutes, and the nausea subsided. Finally, Chloe stood, sucked in clean air deeply and sighed in relief. Her eyes fell on the cigarette she had just discarded, now rolling down the street.

"Ugh," she said, scrunching her face in disgust. "Never again."

CHAPTER TWELVE

Chloe rubbed hard at the syrup on the table, smiling to herself as she lifted the little girl's plate and scrubbed the tiny trail that had already started to harden from the drippings of her fork. She watched through the front window as the fat woman accompanying the girl squeezed herself into the seat of her old car, her weight causing the front end to jump slightly up and down, up and down, as she settled herself behind the wheel. The little girl, hopped up on sugar, scuttled happily into the passenger seat, and immediately propped two white sneakered feet on the dash. Just as quickly, she dropped them, and pulled the seatbelt from over her shoulder and fastened it.

Chloe smiled, watching the woman's mouth move rapidly, then the little girl's downcast expression.

Another happy customer, she thought wryly, wiping up the remains of ice cream that had oozed from the little girl's milkshake glass onto the table just moments earlier.

"Move it, Chloe. There are more tables to bus."

Tony's voice was brusque, and Chloe turned, a snarky reply on her lips. Then something made her stop and she instead shot him a toothy smile.

"Sure thing, boss," she said sweetly, picking up the dishes and cupping them in her arms. She walked past

Tony's shocked face with satisfaction and dumped first the plates, then the cups, into the sink. Wiping her hands dry on her apron, she whispered at Marjorie, who was passing with a tray of plated food, "Kill him with kindness."

"Whatever works," a sweaty-faced Marjorie whispered back, laying her load on the corner of a table while she served the young couple who sat together on the same side, holding hands.

Chloe stifled a laugh and watched as Tony pored over his supply list at one of the empty booths. It'd been six weeks since she resumed her waitressing job, and Tony was still taking revenge on her for leaving him short-handed. At first, he gave her nothing but the overnight shift. Then, when he found how accurate her register counts were, and saw how speedily she tabulated the receipts, he moved her to second shift but gave her some bookkeeping jobs to do. Then, when he saw she seemed to enjoy the bookkeeping, he took that position away and hired a freelancer to do the figuring. Now, a week into paying the contractor what Chloe had been doing for free, he was grumpy, but determined not to show it.

Chloe guessed he'd hold out about another week, before coming back and "ordering" her to do the books again. She didn't mind; it was the one aspect of her job that gave her any enjoyment. Waitressing was so mindless.

She sighed heavily as more customers made their way from the parking lot into the diner.

But it pays the bills—barely, she thought, readjusting her apron and grabbing some menus and glasses for water. A few more weeks and she'd have enough to move from Marjorie's place. She'd found a room for rent down the road from the diner; utilities included and within walking distance of work. It wasn't exactly the life of luxury. But it was

better than being blamed for things. She quickly pushed the
thought from her mind and shoved a fresh pad of paper and
pencil into her apron pocket. No sense dwelling on the past,
she thought, forcing a smile onto her face.

"I got 'em," she said, waving off Marjorie. "Take a break
if you want."

Marjorie smiled gratefully and pushed through the
swinging door into the back.

"Hello, sir, how are you today? I'll be your server,
Chloe," she said brightly, setting down a glass and menu
and arranging a napkin and utensil set neatly on his left.

He turned deeply blue eyes toward her, and Chloe,
taken aback, gaped in surprise. There was something about
his face that seemed so familiar. His eyes, watching her
watch him, glinted in the light and seemed to fade to gray.
Then like that, they were blue again, deep, deep ocean blue.
Chloe's mind raced to place him.

"I'll just have toast," he said, startling her out of her reverie. "Dry toast. No butter."

His voice was gruff, but not unpleasant. In fact, it had a
familiar ring to it, but Chloe couldn't place that either. She
reached for the menu.

"You sure I can't get you something else?" She stared at
his face, chewing the inside of her cheek madly as she ticked
through her memory banks. She was hoping he'd turn his
eyes on her again.

"Dry toast. No butter," he said again, his face fixed
firmly downward, his eyes hidden as they followed the
movement of the water in his glass he shifted ever so lightly
with his fingers. His fingernails were yellowed and thick,
scraggly at the ends as if they hadn't been clipped in years.
But they were clean, weirdly clean and shiny, she saw with
surprise.

Chloe hesitated, watching the sparks of light as they bounced off the waterglass. Then she grabbed the menu and cleared her throat.

"Toast. No butter. Got it."

His black leather jacket was faded from wear and she noticed his hair was longer than she first observed. It was actually tucked beneath his back collar and she wondered how many inches it trailed down his back. There was something black on the seat next to him, but it was partially obscured by his body so she couldn't make out what it was before she stepped away to place his order. She gnawed her cheek again, a nagging haunting memory nipping at her mind. But the more she chased, the more it darted.

She glanced back to the man, and something about his outline, about the way he sat ramrod straight, about his demeanor.

"Does he smell bad?"

The cook's mocking question jolted Chloe and she narrowed her eyes in distaste as she realized he meant her customer. The cook didn't wait for an answer, but instead laughed out loud at his own joke, turning to the slip of paper Chloe handed him and snorting in disapproval. "Yeah, figures. Toast. No doubt, that's all that bum can afford." He tossed the order to the side and went back to flipping eggs on the grill.

Chloe spun on him in outrage.

"Maybe he just likes toast," she said, picking up the order from the floor, where it had floated and shoving it hard against the cook's chest. "What's it to you, anyway? Maybe if you were a better cook, he'd order more than toast."

The cook looked at her with wide eyes.

"I was just joking," he said.

"Yeah, whatever. Move over," she said. "I'll take care of his order."

She surprised herself with her anger. When it came to customers, Chloe was usually one of the first, and loudest, to complain. They were rude, they were demanding, they were cheap with tips; most days, Chloe had to spend several minutes in the bathroom talking herself out of a foul mood before she put on her apron. She'd think about the money, about a home, about maybe one day buying a new car, and how all of that depended on her ability to serve with a smile, so she could get bigger tips.

But the man in the black jacket wasn't rude. He wasn't demanding. And even though Chloe knew dry toast wasn't going to get her a big tip, she didn't think he deserved to be mocked.

Just because someone looks different isn't reason to make fun of them, she thought, casting sidewise looks of indignation at the cook as she yanked two slices of white bread from the bag on the shelf. She dropped them in the toaster and slammed the handle down hard.

On impulse, she grabbed an orange from the hanging fruit basket by the counter, felt it for ripeness, then quickly peeled it and cut it into circular slices, arranging them neatly on a plate. The toast popped and she cut them into triangles, laying them alongside the orange slices and, as an afterthought, grabbed a couple plastic containers of jelly, one strawberry, one grape, and set them carefully in the center of the plate. Finally, she pulled a jug of milk from the refrigerator and filling a shiny clear glass to the top, she balanced the plate on her fingertips and brought it to the man. She placed the plate gingerly before him, then the glass of milk.

"It's on me," she said, when he gazed at her inquisitively.

He watched her for a moment, his eyes turning from blue to gray to green in the span of just a few seconds. His mouth didn't move, but his face seemed to break into a smile just the same. He nodded very slowly, very slightly, and when he did, the light from his eyes took on a life of its own and seemed to dance. Chloe stared in disbelief and wonder at the tiny gold figures with white wings flitting before his face. Then she blinked and they were gone, and all that was before her was an unsmiling man in a black jacket and blue eyes.

"Thank you," he said evenly.

Baffled, still struck by the feeling of familiarity, she spun on her heels and moved to the next table. She swept crumbs into her hand and scrubbed hard with her dishcloth the crusted syrup spots.

More syrup, she thought. *What is it with people and their pancake syrup?*

She grabbed the dirty plates, forks and knives, stacking them expertly in her arm while grasping three glasses by the fingers of one hand. She walked to the sink and dumped the dishes in carefully and, noticing the tray of glasses used to set the tables was nearly empty, she then hurried to the back for clean ones. When she came back, she saw the table with the man in the black jacket was empty.

His food was still there, untouched.

She wondered if he had gone to the bathroom; in fact, she felt sure he had. Then a movement in the parking lot captured her attention and she watched as the man strolled casually across the lot, hands jammed deep in pockets, jacket flapping in the breeze. He wore a floppy black hat, and as Chloe watched, it dawned on her that was probably the object next to him in the booth.

The she felt a surge of anger. He was headed to his car.

"He gets a free meal and doesn't even eat it?" Chloe said it loud enough for other customers to hear, but she didn't care. She flung open the door and stormed across the lot, jogging a few steps to reach him before he slid into the driver seat of an old brown sedan.

"Hey," she said, her face tight, her eyes narrowed. "Why'd you leave without eating? You know, I hafta pay for that, whether you eat it or not."

He turned and looked down, and Chloe took a step back. His eyes swept over her, melting her anger and filling her heart with joy. They were indescribable hues of blue and gray and green, mixing and beaming. She breathed in deeply, filling her lungs with the sudden smell of vanilla, so powerful and vibrant she looked about for a broken bottle of extract.

In that moment, she forgot all but the memory of a little girl, wet with snow and afraid to go home, and the kindly wonderful man who walked with her and listened to her dreams.

"Mr. Xander," she whispered.

She felt the breath catch in her throat and her eyes welled.

He smiled as he slid behind the wheel.

"I left you a tip," he said, starting the engine and rolling down the window as he pulled away. "I always leave tips," he said, with a wave.

She watched as he drove across the lot, catching sight of his license plate right before he pulled from her view.

GODLVSU.

She let go the breath she hadn't been aware she was holding and watched until his car was far in the distance, a small dot headed toward the horizon. A semi-truck turned into the parking lot, blocking Chloe from seeing the road, and with growing annoyance, she waited for the driver to pull past. When he did, the brown sedan was already gone. For several seconds, Chloe stood still, staring at the spot where she last saw his car. Then another truck, this one a passenger size, drove slowly into the light, blocking Chloe's view of the road, once again. She turned to go back inside the diner.

"Chloe."

She looked at the driver peering down at her from the truck window.

"Pastor James." She didn't know what else to say. Her heart jumped, though, as he stepped from the cab and walked to her. He hesitated, then held out his arms and pulled her close.

"How'd you find me?" Chloe dropped her arms and stared curiously at his face. She never told him the name of the place where she had worked, or Marjorie's name, or anybody's name she used to hang out with, for that matter.

He gave a short, tight laugh.

"It wasn't easy," he finally said. "Let's just say I got some tips."

For several seconds, Chloe stood quiet, the words of her last customer coming alive in her mind.

"I would've come sooner," he said, "but I thought you might be too angry to see me."

Chloe nodded. "I was pretty angry."

"You were right, Chloe. You were right about everything, and I just didn't want to hear it. You were right about the stolen money, you were right about Robert being the one who took the money, you were right about getting angry with me for accusing you."

She was about to speak, but he cut her off.

"Wait. I just want to finish. I am really sorry for the way I blamed you and the way I treated you. And I hope you can forgive me." He waited, searching her face. "I really want you to come back to the church, to your job, to teach, to your room—to everything. If you want to, that is. But I need to know you'll forgive me because if you can't, I just don't know what I'll do." He paused again, looking at the sky, then the ground, then around, then back at her face. "I know I'll feel terrible about it, that's for sure."

Chloe smiled, touched by how sorry he sounded.

"Yes, I forgive you. I'm sorry too. I guess I shouldn't have yelled that at you when I was leaving."

"Twice," he said.

"Twice," Chloe laughed. "But yes, I'd love to come back."

The pastor clapped his hands and gave her another quick hug.

"I've got something else to tell you, though," he said, his voice turning serious.

"What?"

He took so long to answer, she started to squirm.

"I think I found your mother," he said.

Chloe's head jolted backward in shock, and she was about to say something when a batch of clouds drifting slowly across the sky captured her attention. She peered closely as they shifted and floated, watching with interest as one seemed to break away from the group and hover for a moment, unmoving. Her eyes turned misty. Chloe saw in its shape a perfectly formed heart.

CHAPTER ONE

"Do it."

Hector stared down the alley at the red truck idling at the light and hesitated. He glanced nervously at his buddies. Leon's face was blank, and his hand was steady as he held out the 9mm, flat against his palm. Gio, next to him swallowed by an overlarge gray hoodie, smiled broadly, his famously large teeth glinting white, even in the darkness. He slapped his hand lightly against his thigh, beating in time to some unknown song playing in his head. Hector cleared his throat and gulped. There would be no getting away from it. He nodded and took the gun, feeling the smooth black-and-silver of the barrel with his fingers before jamming it in his back waistband then pulling his sweatshirt down tight. He felt its cold against his skin and for a moment had a terrible vision of it misfiring and sending a bullet into his spine.

His father's face flashed before his eyes and again, he hesitated. This is not how his father would want him to live.

"Come on, bro. Before the light turns." Leon gave him a push for emphasis. "Gotta pay your dues."

Hector shook himself and took off at an easy pace down the alley, toward the street. Stepping from the shadows, he looked first to the left, then to the right, then again to the left, and finally, at the windows of the truck. He scanned the occupants, just as he had been taught.

The driver—male, middle age, white. The passenger—female, youngish, maybe middle age, also white. He peered as best he could through the tiny window into the back seat but saw no car seats. The woman's window was down a couple inches, and he heard only the faint strumming of a guitar and a quiet male's voice, singing with a twang so thick that Hector grimaced.

He strode around the back of the truck to the driver's side door.

"Get out of the truck! Get out! Now!" He pounded his fist against the window and pointed his gun at the driver's head. The man turned his head in shock and dimly, in the background, Hector heard a woman scream.

The light turned green, Hector panicked, and punched the glass with the butt of his gun. It cracked and the driver pulled back in alarm. Furious, Hector wrapped both hands around the grip and held the barrel at the man's forehead.

"Now! Get out!" He stepped back as the door started to crack open. He leaned around the driver and shouted at the woman. "You! Slide out this way! Let's go!"

The man stepped to the ground, his hands behind his head. Hector motioned him toward the sidewalk then turned the gun toward the woman.

"Now! Now! Now!" From the corner of his eye, he saw lights beaming from a side street.

"Hurry up! Get on the ground! Lay down, faces down!" He watched as the woman scurried to the man's side and they both dropped to the pavement, hands still behind heads, faces turned toward each other. The lights grew brighter.

"Don't you move an inch until you count to 1,000," Hector said, flashing the barrel first at the man, then the woman, then jumping into the truck. The passenger door opened and instinctively, Hector spun the gun to his right.

"Whoa, whoa, take it easy, man." Gio's massive teeth glinted in the light and with a sharp breath, Hector lowered his gun and Gio slid across the seat, followed quickly by Leon.

"Let's go, man, let's go!" Leon slammed the door and Hector hit the gas pedal hard, headlights from an oncoming car flooding the cab. The wheels spun as he raced through the intersection, speeding through the next light and the next, before steering hard to the right, down a side street, then another, until nothing but black showed in his mirror when he checked to the rear.

Laughter filled the truck and Hector, in surprise, looked at his friends.

"Yo, you see that guy's face?" Leon opened his eyes as wide as they could go and then took two fingers of each hand and reached up and pulled them open even more.

"I thought he was gonna drop with a heart attack." Gio choked on his laughs and grabbed Hector's arm hard, as if to steady himself. "Oh man. You did good, though, bro."

"Yeah, you did it, man," Leon said, spreading his legs onto the dash and smiling broadly. He reached over and smacked Hector hard on the shoulder. "You one of us now."

Hector glanced sidewise at Leon but didn't return the smile. He wondered why the thought didn't make him happy.

"Let's pull here for a while, bro, let everything clear," Leon said, pointing through the windshield. "Then we'll drop this with Juan."

Hector followed Leon's gestures and steered into an empty lot, pulling to the shadows of the tree line and shutting off the engine. He watched as Gio rifled through the glove box, pulling out papers and glancing at them, before crumpling them and tossing them out the window. He was about to tell Gio to stop, when Leon whistled, a long, drawn-out whistle, and all six eyes turned to look. Dangling from Gio's fingers was a long silvery chain, and dangling from the end of the chain was a sparkling silver object that gleamed and glittered as it danced.

"What the—" Gio held it still for a closer view. It was a silver Christian cross, dotted with delicate stones of red, yellow, blue, green, and white.

"Dude, are those diamonds?" Leon reached for the cross, but before he could take it Hector leaned over and snatched it from Gio's fingers.

"Gimme that," he said sharply.

It felt warm in his hands and he glanced at it with surprise. For a split second, a spark of light blinded him and he caught a strong, definite whiff of roses. Then the frightened face of the woman he just carjacked slid into mind, and it was as if he could actually hear her high-pitched scream right there in the cab, on the seat next to him. Startled, he shuddered and shoved the cross and chain deep into his front pocket.

"Hey, who says that's yours." It was a statement, more than question, and Hector bit his tongue to hold back the first words that came to mind. He turned to Leon and shrugged, daring him with his eyes to try and take it. They stared that way for several seconds, until Hector turned.

"Come on, dude," Hector said, putting his hands on the steering wheel and feeling the curves of leather with his fingers. "It's my first time. I gotta get something out of it." He hoped Leon would agree. The two never before fought, but Hector had a sneaking suspicion Leon was stronger than he looked.

"Besides," he said, giving Leon a half smile and raising his eyebrow a bit, "whatdoya want a cross for? You're an atheist, man." He waited until Leon smiled back and then laughed.

"Yeah, keep it," Leon said, turning to the window.

Hector breathed a deep quiet sigh of relief. He had no idea why he wanted the cross so much, except maybe it reminded him of his mother and father. He leaned his head against the seat and reached down with his left hand and pinched the cross in his pocket, feeling its hardness and poking his finger into the points of the metal.

My father would not be proud, he thought, closing his eyes and remembering the face of his mother as she peered into his eyes and prayed a prayer of protection over his tired body each evening as he lay in bed.

And neither would she, he thought, his eyes growing damp with sadness.

"Are you all right?"

There was silence for a moment and he asked again.

"Chloe! Are you all right?"

She lifted her head and glanced toward the street, then strained her neck to both sides. The street was empty and she nodded, feeling slightly nauseous as her heart thumped hard against the pavement.

"James," she said, twisting her body into a seated position and waiting until he did the same. "They took your truck." She took deep gulps of air and swallowed hard, willing the nausea to pass.

"Well, you're not hurt, are you?" He stood and reached for her. Gingerly, using his arm as balance, Chloe pulled herself to her feet, then brushed her knees and the back of her pants.

"No. But we should call the cops." Chloe glanced down the darkened streets. "We should probably get out of here too." She watched as he felt in his pockets for something, then turned to her with hands lifted, palms open.

"They got my phone," he said.

Chloe sighed and shook her head.

"Aren't pastors supposed to be protected from this kind of thing?"

He looked at her and grimaced.

"It doesn't work that way, Chloe." He paused and took her by the arm, looking around then pointing at a group of street signs. "Let's head that way."

They walked in silence for several moments, their eyes peeled at the dark corners of the side streets and the black windows of passing buildings. Then he stopped so suddenly Chloe grabbed his hand in fear and she squinted hard at the shadows, wondering what he saw.

"Chloe," he said, turning to her with lips pulled tight. "I think we may have to put off contacting your mother."

Chloe looked at him quizzically. Just hours before he had given her the news that he had located her mother—her biological mother. They had just been discussing when they might reach out to her, and how, and even if—just minutes earlier they had talked about sending a letter. And then their world changed. The image of the gun as it flashed in the light of the street sprung to Chloe's mind and she shivered at how close they had come to death. She reached for his hand and felt for his reassuring squeeze.

Still, she didn't see the connection between the carjacking and contacting her mother.

"All the contact information is in the glove box," James said, as if reading her thoughts.

They continued in silence for several minutes, the sound of their feet clicking on the sidewalk echoing lightly in the darkness.

"Chloe. I have more bad news," he said, breaking the quiet.

He stopped, turned to her, his face pale.

"My cross was in the glove box." He sighed and rubbed his face with his hand. "Oh geesh. It was about the only thing of real value I own."

Chloe looked at him, her eyes unblinking, helpless how to respond.

"It was white gold, had diamonds and other gemstones on it. Real gemstones. I mean, between the gold and the diamonds and the stones, it must be worth thousands. I never had it valued; I'm just guessing. But the diamonds alone . . ." he trailed off, his head shaking slightly. "The diamonds alone," he said again.

Pastor James looked at her and gave another sigh.

"The real value was it was a gift, though."

Chloe looked at him but said nothing. His face was downcast and he looked near tears.

"My uncle gave me that cross after he helped lead me to God. If it hadn't been for him, I never would have become a pastor. I never would have become a Christian, at least, not when I did. I probably would've never quit drinking." He raised his head and turned anguished eyes her way. "I'd be an alcoholic right now. I'm sure of it."

Chloe touched his shoulder gently and shook her head sadly. She was about to speak when he spun and faced her and grabbed both hands in his.

"Pray with me, Chloe. Pray with me now."

Surprised, she nodded and closed her eyes.

"Dear Lord," he said, his voice strangely loud in the empty street, "thank You for keeping us safe during these last minutes of terror. Thank You for letting us come from this attack unharmed, unhurt, mostly untouched—and it's because of Your heavenly protection, we know, that this is why we're unhurt right now. But Father, we ask You to please convict the ones who committed this crime of their sins. Don't let them sleep peacefully tonight, or any night, until they've turned from their path of evil, until they've repented from their acts of evil, and returned the properties they've stolen. Father, we ask specifically that You bring that cross and chain back safely and in one piece to us. You know, Father, how much that cross means to me." James paused, long enough that Chloe peeked and watched as he gulped deep, fighting to control his emotions. After a few moments, he went on and Chloe shut her eyes again.

"We ask, too, that You bring back the truck, Father. It is not mine. It is borrowed and my heart breaks at the thought of having to tell the owner it's been stolen. For his sake, please, Father, convict these thieves and give them no peace until they've returned this truck."

James paused again, breathing deeply and squeezing Chloe's hands between his own.

"Father, it is Your teaching in the Bible that when Joseph was sold into slavery by his brothers, he did not later kill them when he had the opportunity but rather forgave them and said though they intended evil, God intended good—out of their evil plots, God turned it for the good of Joseph, his family, and an entire population. And it is with that same spirit, Father, we say: We forgive these men of their crimes and ask that You use their sins against You for Your glory. We put the outcome of our requests into Your hands, we thank You again for saving us from harm and we praise You for sending Your Son, our Savior, Jesus Christ, to die for our sins so we may have everlasting life. It's in Jesus's name we pray, amen."

"Wow," Chloe said, pulling her hands from his and rubbing them on her thighs. "Your hands are hot."

James flashed her a smile and nodded, wiping his own hands together before resuming their walk.

"I know, mine got warm too."

They turned a corner and at the same time, gasped and ducked their heads. A flash of light, so bright they had to shut their eyes, beamed over them, and they stopped, waiting for the car to pass.

"Geesh," Chloe said, shaking her head hard. "Talk about blinded by the light." Then she scrunched her nose and sniffed.

"Hey, do you smell roses?"

James smiled, then nodded.

"I do. Very strange."

Other Fiction from Fidelis Publishing

Rendezvous with God—
Volume One—Bill Myers

9781735428581 Paperback /
9781735428598 eBook

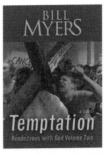

Temptation—Rendezvous with God—
Volume Two—Bill Myers

9781956454024 Paperback /
9781956454031 eBook

Commune: Rendezvous with God—
Volume Three—Bill Myers

9781956454246 Paperback /
9781956454253 eBook

Insight—Rendezvous with God—
Volume Four—Bill Myers

9781956454420 Paperback /
9781956454437 eBook

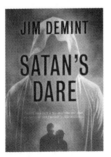

*Satan's Dare—*Jim DeMint

9781735856308 Hardcover /
9781735856315 eBook

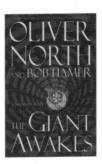

The Giant Awakes: A Jake Kruse Novel—
Oliver North and Bob Hamer

9781956454048 Hardcover /
9781956454055 eBook

A Bellwether Christmas:
A Story Inspired by True
Events—Laurel Guillen
9781956454086 Hardcover /
9781956454093 eBook

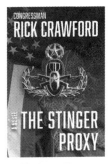

The Stinger Proxy—
Rick Crawford
9781956454215 Hardcover /
9781956454222 eBook

The Inferno—Winston Brady
9781956454260 Paperback /
9781956454277 eBook

The Invisible War: Tribulation
Cult Book 1—Michael Phillips
9781956454321 Paperback /
9781956454338 eBook

The Fear Protocol: A Novel—
Brad Newbold
9781956454550 Paperback /
9781956454567 eBook